Battle of Hearts

"I don't much care for that fellow, Mary. I wish you wouldn't encourage him."

Encourage him? She had done nothing to encourage him. There had been no repartee, no fan play, no fluttering lashes. How dare her husband accuse her of such a thing!

"Lord Blissford was very kind to me in your absence," she began.

"Ha! I'll wager he was. And I'll wager he would like to have shown you even greater kindness, only I have returned to put a spoke in his wheel."

"It is only that I do not like to be made to feel like a toy soldier being fought over by two little boys," said Mary stiffly. "It was not easy making friends on my own and I am grateful to those who were so kind to me when I first arrived."

"I am afraid I am rather a jealous fellow and I hate to share my beautiful wife with other men."

Diamond Books by Sheila Rabe

FAINT HEART
THE IMPROPER MISS PRYM
THE LOST HEIR
LADY LUCK

Lady Luck

Sheila Rabe

DIAMOND BOOKS, NEW YORK

This book is a Diamond original edition, and has never been previously published.

LADY LUCK

A Diamond Book / published by arrangement with the author

PRINTING HISTORY
Diamond edition / December 1992

ISBN: 1-55773-829-7

Diamond Books are published by The Berkley Publishing Group, 200 Madison Avenue, New York, New York 10016.
The name "DIAMOND" and its logo are trademarks belonging to Charter Communications, Inc.

PRINTED IN THE UNITED STATES OF AMERICA

10 9 8 7 6 5 4 3 2 1

For Kerrie

Lady Luck

-One-

THE EARL OF Dorset arrived from France at what he had always supposed to be his town house on an evening in late April. Withers, the butler, opened the door and the staid smile froze on his face. "Your lordship," he stammered.

"So nice to be remembered," said the earl, stepping inside the door and pulling off his gloves. "Is my wife at home?"

The butler licked his lips and swallowed. "I am not sure, your lordship. But your mother is at the theater."

"Where is my wife?" inquired the earl.

"She is possibly at the theater as well," said Withers.

"Possibly? You do not know?"

"I am afraid not, your lordship," replied Withers.

His lordship sighed. He was tired. It had been

1

a long trip. But he had come from France to see Mary and find out what his mother had been so concerned about, and see Mary he would. "Have my trunks brought up to my room immediately," he said, heading up the stairs. "I suppose I shall go to the theater."

"John," he said to his valet as they readied the earl for an evening out, "does it seem to you that Withers has lost some of his mental capacities?"

John shrugged his slender shoulders and removed his master's coat. "I'm afraid I did not notice, your lordship. He did not, I must admit, seem to be expecting us."

"That was my impression as well," said the earl, falling onto a nearby chair. Once down, he had little inclination to stir himself further. It wasn't so much exhaustion that bade him remain as procrastination. "I'd as lief stay right here," he announced. He tapped his chin thoughtfully. "Ah, well. If I wait for the ladies to return, I am bound to fall asleep and that would be most uncivil."

"You are always most civil, your lordship," said the prosaic John, kneeling to pull the boot from the proffered foot.

Within the half hour Jeremy Rufus Arlington, the fifth Earl of Dorset, was attired in the proper evening dress, complete with white waistcoat, silk stockings, and black patent-leather pumps.

2

His coloring was rather ordinary: light brown hair and fair skin. And his build was not large. But in spite of the fact that he was not a tall man, he was well assembled, all sinew and muscle, and he had a nicely turned leg. His lordship also had a straight nose, a strong chin, and a fine pair of brown eyes, so he was accounted by most to be a very good looking young man.

He arrived at the Royal Opera House in Bow Street between acts and found his mother holding court in a private box. A middle-aged fop and a man the earl felt sure must be no more than five years his senior attended her. The earl frowned. How the devil would he be able to learn anything from his mother with these two present? "Good evening, Mother," he said.

The attention of the Dowager Countess Dorset was immediately drawn from the men with her, and a smile lit her face that neither of her suitors had yet been able to inspire. "Jeremy! How delightful. When did you arrive in London?"

"Only this evening," replied her son. "And I came straightaway in search of you."

Her ladyship introduced both her companions with the greatest kindness and, before they knew it, had dispatched them with equal kindness. "Now," she said, patting a chair next to her. "Come sit next to me and let me look at you."

Dorset obeyed, and found himself thinking how little she seemed to change. There were few lines on her face, and the warm brown eyes were as alert as ever. Her body was still youthful and she showed to advantage in her low-cut gown. Louisa, the dowager Lady Dorset, did not look her forty-odd years.

"You look well, dearest," she said, smiling on her son.

"In spite of the worries you have hung on my head," he added. "Really, Mother. Was such a cryptic letter necessary?"

His mother cocked her head and regarded him. "Yes, I believe it was. Else I could never have drawn you from the excitement abroad."

"Napoleon has abdicated. The excitement is ended," said the earl.

"Is it?"

Her son smiled at her. "I am done with my adventuring, as you call it."

"I am glad to hear it," said his mother, "for I feel it is high time you paid attention to your domestic concerns."

"So I gathered from your letter." The earl sighed. For three years he had been able to forget he was a married man. Thanks to his French godmother and an excellent command of the language, he had enjoyed a life of high adventure in the Regent's service, slipping in and out of French-occupied territory with stolen information, enjoying the favors of French trollops, and drinking fine claret. He had often ridden hard, he had just as often played hard. Now he was home. And coming home had been harder than his most dangerous mission, for from the tone of her letter it appeared his mother intended to foist his wife upon him in some uncomfortable manner.

The earl sighed inwardly. Twenty-two had been much too young to be leg-shackled. It had been curst inconsiderate of the fourth earl to break his neck on the hunting field, leaving his son his mountain of gambling debts and a crumbling family mansion. Surely if his sire had to leave him such a legacy, he could have at least had the decency to live a little longer and allowed his son a few more years of freedom.

Of course, handsome as he was, the young earl could have married any number of well-heeled young women. But this marriage had been a bit of a good deed. And with that the earl had had no quarrel. If he had to marry, he could at least do someone else a favor in the process. After all, marriage was a social necessity and one woman would do as well as the next. And he certainly didn't begrudge his wife her season in town. She had seemed nice enough and deserved to kick up her heels a little. But surely she didn't need him dancing attendance on her for that!

The earl rubbed his tired eyes. "What was so urgent that it demanded my immediate presence?" he asked. "I should think with you here to guide her Mary could weather a season in London."

"She is a smashing success," said his mother.

"And I was needed urgently at home to observe my wife's success," guessed the earl.

His mother grinned. "I have raised a very impertinent son," she observed.

The young man returned his mother's grin and leaned back in his seat, regarding her. "I am afraid you have." His grin widened. "I am told I take after you."

Her ladyship changed the subject. "Mary is sponsoring the come-out of a beautiful young cousin," she said.

"That should keep her well entertained," predicted the earl.

"I am afraid it is keeping her more than that," said Lady Dorset. "Poor Mary has found that assisting a young lady with her social debut is not an inexpensive proposition."

"Surely my lawyer could have taken care of any bills that came up. We certainly have the blunt to pay for a few gowns now," said the earl.

"Aubrey is in London as well," said his mother.

"So you wrote me." The earl shook his head. "I can scarcely believe the cub old enough to be turned loose upon London society. It seems only last year he was in school."

"So he was," said the dowager.

Her son blushed at this reminder of his lack of attention to family affairs and cleared his throat. "Quite," he said. "Well, I suppose he is leading his stepsister a merry dance. Is Aubrey the reason I am called home?"

"There are many reasons you have been called home," replied her ladyship. "Have you . . . been home?" she asked.

"Yes, but I did not find Mary."

"Are you, perhaps, hoping I will point her out to you?" guessed her ladyship. The earl blushed and she smiled knowingly. "Very wise, dearest. She has changed much in three years. I doubt you would recognize her."

The earl remembered the scrawny little dowd he had offered for in a moment of chivalry. At sixteen, the only feeling Miss Mary Batten had inspired in her groom was a desire to run. He certainly hoped she had changed.

"Before I show her to you, I should, perhaps, inform you that you are not residing in Grosvenor Square."

"What!" The earl sat up in his chair. "Mother, what kind of jest is this? I was just there."

7

"I am sure you were," said his mother calmly. "But that is not where your wife lives. Do shut your mouth, dearest. I am afraid it does not make you look very intelligent, and if anyone were to be watching, I should hate them to think my son a dolt."

His lordship pressed his mouth into an angry line.

"Mary has rented a town house in Albemarle Street. She felt that as she had both her cousin and Aubrey in her care, it would be kinder to me if she were to house them separately."

The earl's mouth relaxed. "That was most considerate, actually," he said. He looked at his mother, puzzled. "Thus far I can see no reason for you to have summoned me home."

The light left his mother's eyes. Her smile faded and she suddenly looked older. "I am afraid Mary has taken on more responsibility than she realized. I fear that both her younger brother, Aubrey, and her cousin, Miss Tuttle, have proved a most expensive burden. Aubrey has been losing considerable sums of money in some gaming hell, and as I said, the expense of bringing out her young cousin has proved more than Mary bargained for. I think, perhaps, she has not felt comfortable drawing upon your resources, which is why, when she ran out of

pin money, she opened her home for some . . .
select card parties.''

"Card parties?'' The earl had caught the worry
in his mother's voice. ''What sort of card parties?''

Lady Dorset sighed. ''The sort which will
bring her in some extra income.''

The earl's eyes grew. ''A gaming hell?'' he
gasped.

''Heavens, no. It is not so bad as that,'' said her
ladyship. ''What Mary is doing is in nothing but
the best of taste. And I remember when there
was hardly a house of note in the West End
without its faro table. But I also remember that
horrible scandal not so many years ago with
Lady Buckinghamshire. That horrible Gilray and
his nasty drawings!'' Her ladyship shook her
head. ''I am sure I admire Mary's ingenuity, but
I am afraid this is not at all the thing.''

''And did you not tell her so? Good God,
Mother! How could you have let her start such
nonsense?''

''My dear Jeremy, of course I gave the child
my opinion. But I am not, after all, her husband.''

The earl sighed and wished himself back in
France. ''Is she here tonight?''

His mother pointed with her fan across the
theater to a box with two young women in it.
One was a ripely curved, dimpled doll with blue

9

eyes and golden ringlets and a pouting mouth—a conventional beauty. "The child with the yellow curls is your wife's protégée, Miss Amanda Tuttle," said her ladyship.

Sitting next to Miss Tuttle was the most beautiful young woman the earl had ever seen. Her low-cut green satin gown showed off tiny shoulders carved from alabaster. No, not alabaster. Alabaster was beautiful, but it was cold and unyielding. This flesh had the glow of life to it. The lady's décolletage revealed small, plump breasts. She had a long, graceful neck, and on that neck sat a head with a perfect profile and dark curls dusted with copper. The earl stared at her in disbelief. That ravishing creature couldn't be his wife. But there, on that long, lovely neck hung the famous Dorset necklace of emeralds and pearls, the proof of her identity.

As if feeling his eyes on her, the beautiful creature turned her head toward where the earl and his mother sat and looked at him with big brown doe eyes. "My God," breathed the earl.

"No," said his mama. "Your wife."

-Two-

THE EARL STARED in disbelief. "That beautiful woman is my wife?"

"She has changed, hasn't she?" commented his mother.

"You sound as if you knew she would," said the earl accusingly.

"Of course I knew she would," said Lady Dorset. "The child was barely out of the schoolroom when you married her. Women do change."

Well, well. Here was an interesting twist of fate. The good deed he so regretted doing had not been such a mistake after all. He had nobly wed a homely chit he barely knew, all because his mother and hers had been girlhood friends. (And because she would bring a tidy sum to the diminished family coffers, of course.) Now the orphaned heiress who had been given title and position had rewarded her benefactor by turning

11

into a beauty. His lordship smiled, well pleased with the bargain.

His mother smiled also, but her smile showed traces of irritation. "So now that Mary has turned out to be a beauty, you think, perhaps, she is worthy of your attention?"

His thoughts, verbalized, seemed crude, indeed. "Mother, I have been busy with the war," he said.

"Ah, yes. The war."

Her tone of voice made his excuse sound as feeble as it was. Even the most patriotic of grooms would hardly leave his bride without so much as consummating their marriage. Well, she had been young and innocent, the earl reasoned. She had barely known him. It would have been most ungentlemanly to demand anything of the poor girl. But now . . .

"I suppose you think you will stroll into her bedroom tonight and she will welcome you with open arms," divined his mother.

The earl opened his mouth to speak, then thought better of it, instead folding his arms and studying his elegantly shod feet. He had thought at least to move into his own town house. How would it look to the ton if the Earl of Dorset stayed with his mother while his wife lived in a separate establishment? But he suddenly realized how very unlikely it would be that he could descend on the woman who had received no more than half a dozen letters from him in the last three years and even be welcomed in her drawing room, let alone her bedroom or any other bedroom in the house.

For the first time the earl found himself desirous of his wife's good opinion. And fool that he'd been, he'd done nothing these past three years to deserve it. Why the devil hadn't he written her more often? What would it have cost him but a little time?

He ceased regarding the toes of his pumps and looked across the room again. The beauty was looking at him curiously and he found himself blushing. He tried to smile his most charming smile, but it seemed only half his lip would lift and he cursed himself for a silly clunch, not realizing how endearing his lopsided grin looked.

The incredible creature gave him a polite smile, then slowly turned her face back toward the stage as the lights were dimmed, giving him one last look at her perfect profile before the audience settled into darkness. The earl sighed. An interesting twist of fate, indeed, he thought bitterly. Here he was married to the most beautiful woman in London, and he would be spending his first night home with his mother!

* * *

The earl was slow to wake the following morning, as if wishing to postpone what could only be an embarrassing interview. He finally tired of lying abed and summoned his valet. "Make me look irresistible, John," he said. "For I go to see my wife this morning and I wish to make a good impression."

"You have never yet failed to make a good impression on the ladies, your lordship," remarked John.

"Yes, but this is different. This particular lady has good reason to bear me a grudge."

John shook his head. "You sent her that fine French gown for her birthday, and Christmas last you gave her a pug dog. I should say you have been a most considerate husband."

"Gowns and pug dogs cannot atone for a lack of letters." The earl shook his head. "I have been a great fool," he said. "And I do not relish this first meeting with Mary."

"Then perhaps the brown coat?" suggested John. "The color is most complimentary."

The earl smiled ruefully. If only the right-colored coat were all that was required to impress a wife. Well, it was a start.

Feeling it would never do to visit his wife empty-handed, the earl stopped at Gunther's and purchased a box of fine and common sugarplums. Thus armed, he found himself nervously clearing his throat and walking past the butler into her drawing room.

She was alone. She had obviously been curled up on the sofa with a book, which was now laid aside, and she was slipping a dainty foot into her slipper. For an instant the earl had a vision of a tender reunion. He would softly say, "I am returned, Mary." Her eyes would fill with tears and she would beckon him to come sit next to her and tell her all about his adventures the last three years.

It was, sadly, not a prophetic vision. Out of nowhere a small, brown thing came to make a growling attack on his new Hessians. The earl let out a startled yelp and dropped his box of sugarplums. The lid bounced off and his offering scattered about his feet. Trying not to step on any, he shook his foot in an effort to remove the tiny monster's teeth.

"Oh, dear!" cried Mary, and ran to scoop up the angry animal. "No, Rufus!" She grabbed the little dog and came up blushing. "I am so sorry," she said.

"No harm done," lied the earl, resisting the urge to examine his tooth-marked boot. He knelt to pick up the scattered sugarplums.

"Please do not bother, my lord. Jeffries can do that." She moved to ring for the butler.

"No. Let us not be bothered with the servants just now," said his lordship. He scooped the sweets into the box. He smiled apologetically up at her. "I shall bring you a bigger box next time." She smiled back nervously and the earl cast about his mind for something to say. Somehow "I am returned" no longer seemed appropriate.

"Won't you sit down?" she offered.

The earl sat. The pug growled at him from its mistress's arms. He tried to smile at it. "Rufus, eh?" he said.

Mary blushed. "I felt, somehow, I should name him after you," she said.

"I hope it was not his disposition that inspired you to do so," said his lordship.

She smiled. She was even more beautiful when she smiled. "No," she said. She looked down at the little dog and her look was almost wistful. "I thought it would be a nice gesture."

A nice gesture. She had been thinking of him in his absence. Fool! Stupid, selfish fool that he was, he had rarely thought of her.

It was now the earl's turn to contribute something to the conversation, but he found himself strangely lacking in contributions. Under the circumstances anything flirtatious would be grossly inappropriate. And any small talk about the weather would be equally out of place. Best to come right to the point, tell his wife he intended to take up residence in Albemarle Street. How to broach the subject? "I was surprised to find you not staying in our family town house," he began.

"Your mother has, most likely, told you my stepbrother is with me, and a young cousin who is making her social debut. I did not like to discommode her with so much confusion, and I did not feel right asking her to give her home up."

"You are the new Lady Dorset," pointed out the earl. "I am sure my mother was expecting to give the house up to you."

His wife merely shook her head.

"This plan to come to London was rather sudden, was it not? I don't remember you writing me of it." The earl flushed guiltily even as he said this, remembering the few timid letters he had first received from his new bride. With time their number had dwindled into silence.

Mary looked upset by this comment. "Would you rather I had not come to town?" she asked.

"Oh, no. No. I should certainly want you to be happy. Most ladies are happiest when they can spend a season in town." He shrugged helplessly. "I should have suggested it."

"You had other things on your mind," said his wife. Kind words. But there was something about the tone. Were they underlaid with resentment?

17

"Yes, well." Was it getting warm in this room? The earl pulled at his cravat. "I am afraid I was a very poor correspondent while I was away."

His wife smiled at him. It was not a particularly warm smile. "Yes, I am afraid you were, my lord."

My lord! Why must she keep calling him "my lord"? "Don't you think it would be more proper if you were to call me Jeremy?" he suggested.

"Of course," she agreed primly. "And where will you be staying while you are in London, Jeremy?" she asked politely.

The earl's eyes widened. "Why, here, naturally."

Mary colored up and dropped her eyes. "Of course," she murmured. "How silly of me. I shall have a guest room—"

"The bedroom adjoining yours shall do nicely," said the earl firmly. He couldn't blame the chit for wishing to make him suffer. But really. This was the outside of enough! Mary looked extremely nervous. Her face glowed ember red and she swallowed several times. What the devil did she think he meant to do, cut her throat? Perhaps she would think that preferable to a night spent in his bed. "My dear girl," he said frostily. "I have no intention of forcing my attentions on you, if that is what worries you. But as I am your

18

husband, I think it only natural I be given an adjoining bedroom. If the thought of my nearness so frightens you, you may lock your door." Mary looked about to cry and he had no desire to cope with feminine tears. Their interview had already been uncomfortable enough. He rose. "I had best be on my way. I have several things to do this afternoon before returning."

She rose as well, the little dog still in her arms. "I am sure you have much to do after being gone so long," she said. "You will, most like, wish to dine at your club tonight?" It was a plea.

Good God, what a welcome! Well, it was no less than he deserved. The least he could do was to give his wife one last evening of freedom. "Yes, I shall dine with friends this evening," he said. "I shall look forward to seeing Aubrey again, and to meeting your protégée." He reached to take her hand and kiss it, or at least bow over it. The little dog growled. Beauty and the beast, thought Dorset irritably.

"Rufus!" scolded Mary.

"I can hardly blame him for being devoted to you," said the earl, smiling at her. And if I had been as devoted, perhaps I, too, would now be taken so lovingly in your arms, he thought as he left. This was, indeed, a sorry way to begin a marriage.

* * *

Mary watched him go from the drawing-room window. "Ah, Rufus," she murmured. "He is as handsome as ever, is he not? Why must he return just now and stir up all those old feelings when I already have so much to worry about?" She sighed and blinked back a tear and let the curtain fall back in place.

"Who was just here?" asked a soft voice from the door.

Her ladyship gave a start. "Amanda," she said. "I did not hear you come in." She turned a bright smile on her protégée.

Miss Tuttle was not so easily distracted. "I only caught a glimpse of him from the stair, but he looked quite handsome," she said, settling herself on a chair.

"He is," agreed Mary.

"Well?" Amanda looked expectantly at Mary.

"He is my husband, only just returned from France."

"How exciting! He can, most like, tell us of all the latest styles."

"He can, most like, tell me to stop my Tuesday-evening card parties," muttered Mary.

Miss Tuttle had very fine hearing. "Stop your card parties? Nonsense. Why should he wish to do that? They are all the crack. The Duchess of

20

Goldborough herself told me she vastly enjoys coming here to play."

"Yes, I am sure she does. But I am not sure that the approval of the Duchess of Goldborough will guarantee my husband's approval. In fact, I am afraid he would very much consider the duchess to be a most inappropriate example for a girl making her come-out."

"Oh, pooh!" scoffed Amanda. "I think she is ever so much fun. And I adore watching her play faro. There is nothing she would not do to keep in the game." Amanda lowered her voice to a conspiratorial whisper. "Why, the other night I heard her offer the Earl of Avonleigh a kiss if he would loan her fifty pounds."

"That was not all she offered," muttered Mary.

"What else did she offer?" asked Miss Tuttle innocently.

"Never mind," said Mary. "I am sorry you were a witness to such improper behavior. Perhaps it will be as well if these evenings are brought to an end."

"But how I shall finance the rest of Amanda's season if they are is a most worrisome mystery," Mary confessed later to Randall, her lady's maid and confidante.

Randall took a hairpin from her mouth and pinned up a ringlet. "You will think of something," she said confidently. "You always have.

And things always turn out. Only look how well they turned out when you thought to write Lady Dorset after your papa and stepmama were killed in that accident."

"Yes. I became a bride with no husband for three years," said Mary cynically.

"Better than to be a bride with a husband such as Mr. Amhearst," said Randall.

"Oh, dear, yes," agreed Mary. "Poor Mr. Amhearst. He was so very fat. And always bosky before dinner was even half over."

"He had designs on you," said Randall.

"He had designs on our land," corrected Mary. "He and Papa used to talk about uniting our families. And our lands."

"Well, there is still his daughter. Perhaps she can marry your stepbrother," said Randall, happily settling everyone's problems.

Mary laughed. "Randall, Randall. You have a way of working everything 'round to a happy ending."

"Things usually do work their way 'round to one," insisted Randall. "Which is why I don't understand you worrying about paying for Miss Amanda's come-out. Now that the earl is back, he will take care of things."

Mary's face took on a stubborn look. "I cannot have Jeremy bailing me out. It would hardly be fair. After all, it was not his idea for me to launch my cousin. Oh, dear. I do wish now I had not let Aunt Eloise pester me into doing this."

"But what could you have done? The poor Tuttles could hardly launch her in style on their small income, and with five more daughters left to go after her."

Mary sighed. "I wish I was back at the Manor."

"I am sure his lordship does not," said Randall. "You have become so lovely he will want everyone to see you. You are a credit to him."

Mary bit her lip. "I doubt he will think my friendship with Lord Blissford a credit to him." The corners of her maid's mouth turned up at this. Mary caught sight of the teasing smile reflected in her looking-glass mirror and gave her maid a haughty look. "It is only a friendship."

"A very friendly friendship," agreed Randall.

"I have done nothing improper," said Mary primly.

"Of course, my lady," said Randall in tones that said, *And I hope you may convince your husband of that.*

Mary sighed. "I must face the facts. There is very little I have done since coming to London of which my husband will approve. I should not be at all surprised if he sent me packing back to the Manor immediately, and kept me there alone another three years."

"Now that you have turned into such a beauty, I doubt he will send you back alone," said Randall sagely.

Mary smiled at her abigail. "You are such a treasure. What I would ever have done without you these past four years I don't know."

Randall grinned broadly at this compliment. She stepped back and admired her handiwork. Lady Dorset would look lovely tonight, receiving her visitors in a gown of Skeffington-brown satin, a matching ribbon threaded through her hair. Around her neck was a simple pearl necklace, and matching pearl droplets dangled from her ears.

"Shall I do?" asked Mary.

"Oh, yes," said Randall admiringly. "How any of the men tonight will be able to concentrate on the cards with you looking so fine I don't know."

"Let us hope they cannot," said Mary. "It could be my last night running a gambling establishment and I wish to win a great deal of money."

Not being especially wanted at his town house, the earl had killed a creditable amount of his afternoon shopping in Bond Street. After purchasing a new snuffbox and some Imperial water, he had checked in at White's and Brooks's.

He was a member of both. He had seen several acquaintances, each of whom had congratulated him on his excellent taste in choosing a wife. The earl accepted their congratulations, all the while suspicious that he was already becoming a laughingstock because of his wife's activities.

During his rambles he had kept an eye out for his cousin Sir Percival Vayne, half expecting to see him in Lock's choosing a hat or at Fribourg and Treyer, consulting with those supreme tobacconists about snuff mixtures. He had not, however, encountered his cousin, which was just as well for Sir Percival. After calling at Sir Percival's town house and finding him absent, the earl began to suspect old Percy had heard he was in town and was avoiding him. This did nothing to improve the earl's mood.

"Is Percy in town?" he asked his mother casually as they dined that evening.

"Yes. You have not seen him?"

Jeremy shook his head. "I begin to suspect he is avoiding me."

The dowager was strangely quiet.

"Mother. Has Percy been a party to Mary's schemes?"

Her ladyship paid close attention to the cutting of her turbot. "Jeremy, I wish you would not ask me anything further about Mary. I feel quite badly about what I have already told you."

The earl laid down his fork. "He has, the swine!"

"Now, Jeremy," began his mother.

"Really, Mother. I asked Percy to keep an eye on Mary while I was gone. Is this his idea of keeping an eye on her, letting her come to town and set up her own establishment, turning the place into a gaming hell?"

"It is not a hell," said his mother.

"Faugh." The earl threw down his napkin.

"Jeremy, where are you going?" demanded his mother.

"I am going home. To my wife."

The dowager watched him go. "Oh, dear." She sighed. "I hope Mary can forgive me."

-Three-

THE EARL ARRIVED in Albemarle Street in time to see several people entering the house his wife had taken.

The real reason why his wife had wished him occupied at his club this evening suddenly dawned on him, and he stalked up to the door and followed the others inside. The man who opened the door was not the distinguished, gray-haired butler he had encountered earlier that day. This fellow did not look to the earl like anyone who should be allowed into an upper-class establishment, much less left manning the door to one. He had narrow eyes and a nose that leaned to the side as only a previously broken proboscis could. The man looked critically at his lordship. "And who might you be, sir?" he asked.

The insolence! "I might be the Earl of Dorset," snapped the earl, removing his cape with a flourish.

"Ha! That's a good one. Everyone knows he's in France with the frogs."

"Well, he isn't anymore. He is here. And now that he is, you may leave." The man looked at the earl as if he had not understood. "You are dismissed," said his lordship. "Get out."

The earl walked past the gaping porter and followed the hubbub upstairs to a suite of salons on the first floor. He stopped in the doorway of the first room and surveyed the scene before him through narrowed eyes.

The room was done in shades of blue. Powder-blue brocade covered the sofa that sat along the wall. The Aubusson carpet and the velvet drapes were of a slightly deeper shade. Everything from the furniture to the marble mantel over the hearth bespoke elegance. The room was equipped with a number of small tables and chairs, which would soon be used for card playing.

At the far end of the room sat a green felt table. Next to it stood a foppish-looking young man with brown curls and a beaky nose holding a deck of cards, ready to man his station as faro dealer. He seemed nervous, looking around the room as if expecting to see someone or something unpleasant. His roaming eyes found the earl and the color fled from his face. He sank onto his chair, the cards falling from his hand onto the table.

The earl turned to a nearby footman. "I have just dismissed the porter. Please be so good as to take his place at the front door and tell all callers her ladyship is indisposed tonight and will be unable to entertain visitors."

For only a moment the footman hesitated. The whole staff had been buzzing with the news that the earl had returned to town and had been to call on her ladyship earlier that day. This could be no one else. "Very good, sir," he said, and left to do the master's bidding.

Mary had seen her husband's entrance, and the look on his face. With a weak smile she watched him cross the room to the faro table. "Oh, my!" she exclaimed, trying to sound gay. "Look who has returned!" She excused herself from her guests and ran across the room.

"Percy," his lordship was saying. "How good to run into you. I looked for you earlier today."

Sir Percival ventured a smile. "Well, here I am," he said. "Good to see you, old fellow. When did you arrive?"

"Never mind that," hissed the earl, done playing games. "What is going on here? And why do

I find you a part of it? I asked you to keep an eye on Mary. Is this how you do it, by running a bloody faro bank for her?"

"I tried," protested Sir Percy. "Really . . ."

"Jeremy!" His lordship found his arm taken and his wife at his side, smiling up at him, waiting for him to kiss her cheek.

He blushed and did so.

"How wonderful to see you. I thought your business would keep you away tonight," she said.

"As you see, it did not," said the earl, also smiling. "Come, my dear. We must say good-bye to our guests." His wife looked at him with pleading eyes, but he merely shook his head and led her back to the cluster of chattering people.

"So you have returned to us at last," said a beautiful fair-haired woman, smiling. "And just in time to enjoy the night's festivities."

"Duchess, I am sorry to rob you of your evening's enjoyment, but I am afraid my wife will be unable to entertain tonight." There was a polite murmur of protests. "As you can see," he said, indicating his pale cousin, "her faro dealer is feeling indisposed."

"So it would appear," agreed the Duchess of Goldborough. "Poor boy. Ah, but we can content ourselves with hazard or whist."

"I am afraid my wife is not feeling all the thing, either," confided the earl. And, indeed, Mary looked nearly as pale as Sir Percival. "So inconvenient for you all," said Lord Dorset, walking his incensed guests to the door. "I am so sorry."

One man with fair locks and a mischievous smile took Mary's hand. "I am sure you will be feeling more the thing very soon," he said.

She smiled at him gratefully and the earl frowned. He didn't know Lord Blissford very well, but he knew enough about him to be displeased with the friendship that he saw between Blissford and Mary.

His wife blushed under her husband's scrutiny and said a timid farewell to her guests. When they were gone, she clamped her lips shut and walked back into the room.

"I am sorry to start off on the wrong foot," he apologized. "But, really. This is not at all the thing, Mary." He looked accusingly at his cousin who flushed and looked helplessly back at him. "As Percy should have told you."

"Oh, please don't blame Percy," said Mary, all anger gone. "This was my idea. I . . ." She faltered.

"Found yourself in dun territory?" supplied her husband.

Mary bit her lip and turned her back. "I am afraid I met with some unexpected expenses."

"I am sure they were nothing we could not afford to pay," said the earl. "Mary, I do not mean to scold you, but we have a position to maintain, a reputation. My family has never been involved in any scandal."

"I was not doing anything scandalous," protested Mary.

"She's right," added Sir Percival. "All in the best of taste. Better Suppers than Boodle's."

"I suppose that criminal guarding the door is meant to be a reflection of my wife's good taste?"

Sir Percival was about to reply when his attention was distracted by a rustling noise in the doorway. A besotted grin suddenly appeared on his face and the earl turned in irritation to see what unwanted guest had gotten past his guard at the door.

"Where is our company?" asked Miss Amanda Tuttle.

"They are gone," said Mary. "Amanda, this is my husband. I am sure you have heard me mention Jeremy to you?"

Miss Tuttle curtsied. "I am very pleased to finally meet you. Mary said you were away in France and we would, most likely, not see you."

The earl bowed over her hand. "I am no longer needed in France," he said.

Miss Tuttle seemed unsure how to answer this. "Oh," she said. She looked around the deserted room. "What shall we do now?"

A very good question, indeed. Lord Dorset wanted nothing more than to spend the evening in the company of his wife, getting to know her, promising her that his actions this night would not make her a social outcast. Indeed, if a particular one of her guests never spoke to her again, it would be fine with him. He also had a burning desire to grab his cousin Percy by the cravat and threaten him with all manner of bodily harm for so neglecting his duty. Of course, in all fairness he knew he could hardly rail at Percy when he himself had been so neglecting in his duties as a husband. And here was this curst Miss Tuttle expecting to be entertained. The earl resigned himself to a long, frustrating evening. "I suppose, as this was to be an evening of cards, we had best play whist."

"We could play at faro," suggested Miss Tuttle. "Just the four of us!"

The earl looked with distaste at the green felt table.

"I think, perhaps, whist would be more to our liking," said Mary diplomatically, seating herself at one of the small tables. "Will you partner me, Percy?"

Sir Percy said he would be delighted and he and the other two joined her.

It did not take Lord Dorset long to discover why Miss Tuttle preferred games of chance to ones of skill. Her understanding of the game was not great and she had a most irritating habit of discarding her valuable trump cards when her partner had already taken the trick. He noticed his wife, on the other hand, was an excellent player. Under the circumstances he found her cleverness hard to admire.

The evening seemed to stretch on forever, until the earl feared they would never see the end of it. It was with great relief that he greeted the arrival of the supper cart at ten-thirty. And on seeing the barrel of oysters and the hot pheasant, he realized how little dinner he had had.

Eating restored his good humor—until his wife announced her intention of retiring and suggested that Miss Tuttle might wish to do so as well. She rose, Miss Tuttle as her shield, and before her husband could barely wish her good night, retreated to her bedroom.

He watched her go, the black cloud of extreme irritation settling over him once more.

"Now, Jeremy," said his cousin as soon as the door was closed behind the ladies. "I know what you are thinking. But really, it ain't my fault.

What could I do? I told her I didn't think this was quite the thing."

"And then helped her do it by acting as her faro dealer," accused the earl.

"Thought if she was going to do this, I'd best be around to keep an eye on things," said Sir Percy.

"Who even suggested such a thing to her?" demanded Dorset.

"I ain't sure," said his cousin. "But I think it was Blissford."

"Blissford." The earl spat the name. "Why the devil did you let her encourage Blissford?"

"Well, I . . . Now, wait a second. You never said to lock her in her room. Pretty gel like that. Bound to pick up some admirers. And you didn't seem to care one way or the other when you left."

"That was before . . . Oh, never mind," finished the earl crossly.

His cousin looked at him knowingly. "Before she turned out to be a diamond of the first water," he finished. "Well, and who'd have thought it," he continued consolingly. "She was curst homely when you married her."

His lordship sighed and put his chin in his palm. "I am not getting off to a very good start as a husband," he announced.

His cousin nodded in agreement.

"I don't think she likes me even the smallest bit," Dorset continued.

"Oh, I think she likes you well enough," said his cousin. "Haven't heard her say a single unkind thing about you."

"That hardly means she cares for me. It simply means she is too kind to say what she really thinks," said the earl. "And with all these people about I don't know how I'll get a chance to win her good opinion." He looked around as if just noticing someone's absence. "Where, by the way, is Aubrey?"

"In a hell, most like," said Percy. "He's into some deep play. Rather a havey-cavey lot."

"Well, now, who introduced him to all that?" demanded Dorset.

Percy held up his hands in protest. "It wasn't me!"

The two men settled into silence and Percy smiled at some pleasant daydream. "Miss Tuttle is a pretty little thing, ain't she?" he murmured.

His cousin cocked an eyebrow at him. "Cupid's bow has struck, has it?" Percy blushed and the earl laughed. "If you're so mad for her, I wish you would propose straightaway. Then she can go home and begin to plan her trousseau and

I shall have my wife to myself." His cousin did not smile at this sally. "What is it, old fellow? You don't like her that well?"

Percy shook his head. "I like her very well."

"Then what's to do? Offer for the girl and be done with it. You've got plenty of blunt, you've got a title. What more could she want?"

"Mayhill," said Percy miserably.

"The cub?" The earl was amazed. "What the devil would she see in a stripling such as Aubrey?"

Percy shrugged, bravely pretending nonchalance. "The fellow's much better looking. Got that dark hair like Mary's. Got a fine leg."

"So do you," pointed out his lordship.

Percy shook his head. "He's got a face like his sister's, too. Nice nose."

"There is nothing wrong with your nose," said Dorset.

His cousin looked accusingly at him.

"I am not jesting. There is nothing wrong with your nose. It is a fine, Roman nose."

"You heard that from my mother," accused Sir Percy.

The earl blushed. He remembered on many occasions hearing his aunt refer to his cousin's fierce beak as a fine example of Rome at its best.

"Well, she was right," he insisted. "There is nothing wrong with you."

"I ain't half so charming as your brother-in-law."

"You ain't half so wild, either," said the earl.

Percy sighed. "Ah, well. Never was much in the petticoat line anyway." He rose. "Look at all the trouble it is. Look at you."

Now it was his lordship's turn to sigh. "Watching me should be enough to warn any man away from parson's mousetrap."

His cousin could think of nothing to say to this and both men sat for some time in dejected silence before Sir Percy took himself off home.

The earl was in no hurry to go up to his lonely bedroom, so he wandered into the library, poured himself a glass of claret, and settled in with a book. Sometime in the wee hours something awakened him from a doze. He rubbed his eyes, scratched his head, and looked at the clock on the mantel. Four o'clock. Time for bed.

The earl was halfway to his room when a faint noise from downstairs caught his attention. Cautiously he made his way back down the stairs. He stood poised in the hallway, listening. There it was again! He lightly ran toward the back of the house.

He heard the sound again. He looked to his

left. It had come from that room, and it sounded suspiciously like someone had tripped over something. His heart began to pump violently, and he stealthily cracked the door and peered in. There, in the dim glimmer of early morning, he saw an open window, and a figure tiptoeing across the room.

-Four-

MR. AUBREY MAYHILL made his way to the door with as much stealth as a slightly bosky man could. Slowly he opened it and stuck his head out. That was when he found himself grabbed by the cravat and yanked nose to nose with a man who looked remarkably like his brother-in-law. Aubrey gulped and blinked and tried to bring the face of his attacker into focus. "Dorset?" he stammered.

"Be quiet, cub," murmured the earl, "and be so good as to precede me back into the room."

Aubrey did as he was bade and stood waiting meekly while his lordship lit a candelabra.

The earl placed it on a small table next to Aubrey, throwing his flushed face in the light, then retreated to a chair and made himself at home. From the shadows his disembodied voice asked, "Do you now prefer entering a house through the window rather than the door?"

Aubrey scratched his head. "The door was locked," he said, and by the tone of his voice it was clear he found this circumstance extremely puzzling.

"I am sorry if you were inconvenienced," said the earl. "Where have you been?"

"Oh, just out and about," replied Aubrey airily.

"Winning money?" asked his lordship.

Aubrey shook his head regretfully. "Had the devil's own luck tonight. Besides, I think the club has an unfair hazard table. Can't prove it yet, mind you. But I'm sure they're scalpers."

"I am sure you are correct," agreed the earl. "And how do you intend to pay for your losses tonight?"

"They have my vowel," said Aubrey.

"I certainly hope you have some money stuffed in a stocking upstairs somewhere," said the voice from the shadows. "For I shall not be paying your debt for you."

"Here now," objected Aubrey. "I wouldn't dream of asking you."

"I am sure you wouldn't," murmured the earl. "And your sister won't have the blunt to bail you out, either, as she is no longer running a gambling establishment."

"What's this?" objected Aubrey. "She was all the crack! Why the devil would she give it up?"

"Because I wish her to," replied the earl.

"Of all the stiff-rumped . . ." muttered Aubrey. He frowned at the shadowy form, trying to bring it into focus.

The earl blew out the candles. "Good night, cub," he said, and sauntered out of the room, leaving Mr. Mayhill once more to weave his way through the darkness.

The following morning at breakfast Aubrey was looking tired and sulky. If the earl noticed his brother-in-law's bad mood, he gave no sign of it, choosing instead to attempt a conversation with his wife. But she was not at her best, whether because she was not a lover of mornings or because she was concerned for her brother Dorset couldn't be sure. After the subject of how well she slept and what she planned to do that day had been exhausted, he gave up and excused himself from the table.

Aubrey watched him go, a surly expression on his face. "Well," he said. "I didn't remember Dorset as such a stiff-rumped, high-in-the-instep fellow. I must say I am disappointed in him."

"Why, Aubrey! How can you be so unfair as to judge Jeremy simply from his breakfast conversation. I did not think he seemed so very high in the instep."

"You did not talk to him last night," said her bother.

"You saw Jeremy last night?"

Aubrey nodded. "He won't give me the money to pay my debts. Can you imagine such a thing? I'll have to go see the cent percenters. God knows where it will all end. But it will be Dorset's fault."

"Oh, dear." Mary looked worried. "Well, I have a little money put by."

Aubrey shook his head. "No. I shouldn't expect you to be always pulling me out of the River Tick. Besides, Dorset said you can't loan me any blunt."

"What! That is ridiculous. If you need money . . ."

Aubrey looked pitifully at his sister. "I thought my luck was in. I'm sure I can repay you by the end of the week."

"Don't worry about it, dearest," said Mary.

"If Dorset finds out . . ." Aubrey left his sentence unfinished.

"I wish you wouldn't worry yourself anymore on the subject," said Mary, rising.

Her brother, too, rose and followed her out of the room. "He'll make our lives miserable now he's returned," he predicted.

"I am sure Jeremy has no wish to do such a thing," said Mary firmly.

44

"He may have no wish to do such a thing, but he will anyway," said Aubrey. "I'm going to go look for lodgings today."

Miss Tuttle took the news of Aubrey's imminent departure hard. "Now we shall never see him," she said mournfully to Mary that afternoon.

"Oh, I am sure he'll come 'round for a visit quite often," Mary reassured her. In fact, she thought, he'll most likely never leave. What could he possibly afford with his pockets so sadly to let?

Amanda sighed. "I suppose we won't play faro anymore, either."

"We can still play silver loo. And, of course, there is Lady Wexford's card party in two weeks."

Aubrey had sauntered into the drawing room in time to hear the last part of the ladies' conversation. He snorted contemptuously. "Small stuff," he said.

"But you still plan to accompany us, don't you?" asked Amanda.

Aubrey nodded. "Oh, yes. It will probably be boring as dust, but I shall come. Of course," he added casually, "you will have to send word to remind me. Once I have my own lodgings, I shall be very busy."

"It won't be half so fun with you gone," said Amanda.

"Oh, I shall pop 'round every so often just to see how you go on," Aubrey assured her.

"I may not be here," she informed him. "I shan't wait around simply in the hopes of seeing you."

"Than I shall have to content myself with seeing you whenever you are out," said Aubrey.

"I shall be out tonight," Amanda announced.

"The ball," guessed Aubrey. "I'll wager you thought I'd forgotten."

"Now that you are such a busy and important man with your own lodgings, you might," said Amanda sarcastically.

Mary listened to their banter and smiled wistfully.

"Does the earl accompany you to the ball?" asked Randall as she helped her mistress dress for dinner that night.

"I hope so," said Mary. A vision of herself and her husband engaged in the same kind of lively banter she had heard earlier that day between Amanda and Aubrey twirled across her mind.

She came down to dinner and the combined efforts of her and her maid were rewarded by an appreciative smile from her husband. "Green is a lovely color for you," he said. "I hope you shall reserve me a dance."

She smiled shyly. "Of course," she replied.

Miss Tuttle looked at her patroness with the

complacency of youth. "You look very lovely tonight," she said.

Mary smiled on the girl. "As do you," she said.

Amanda preened, admiring the pink-beribboned gown. "I think this color is very becoming to me," she said. "Do you think Aubrey will like it?"

"I am sure he will," Mary assured her.

At that moment Aubrey joined them in the dining room. He smiled at Amanda appreciatively and tossed her a careless compliment.

"Did you find lodgings?" she asked.

Aubrey felt his brother-in-law's cynical gaze on him and blushed. "Nothing that suited me," he said. "I shall have to wait till I'm a little more plump in the pocket," he added.

Talk at dinner centered mainly around the ball—who was expected to attend, who Amanda thought would wish to dance with her, what the other women would possibly be wearing. "Is it nearly time to leave?" she asked at last.

Mary smiled indulgently at her, and Dorset, too, smiled. "Yes. I think it is time we were leaving," he said. He watched the butler help the ladies into their cloaks, fighting the urge to wrap Mary in hers himself and then wrap his arms around her.

The four hastened through a spring drizzle

and into the crested carriage, and within minutes found themselves in a long line of carriages waiting to pull up in front of Lord Newbury's town house. Amanda fidgeted as they made their slow progress. "The ball will be well in progress by the time we get inside," she complained.

"That may be. But I am sure for many young men the ball won't really start until you are there," said Mary consolingly. "And we'll still have many hours to dance once in the ballroom." Her husband smiled at her and she blushed, feeling strangely self-conscious.

Once inside, relieved of their wraps and the social obligation of greeting their host and hostess, they were free to enjoy themselves. Several young men greeted Miss Tuttle, asking to have their names written on her dance card. Dorset turned to his wife. "Will you give me this first dance before your dance card is filled?"

Mary smiled at him. "As I am now a matron, I think there is little danger of that." But she obliged him. The musicians were playing a country dance, hardly a proper dance for making love to a lady. But it was a beginning, and Lord and Lady Dorset hopped and twirled with the other guests and enjoyed themselves quite well. "That was great fun," said the earl when they were finished. "But not as enjoyable as a waltz. Perhaps you will save me one?"

"Of course," said his lady politely. "I should be happy to do so."

Dorset smiled, feeling he was making good progress in wooing his wife. The approach of Lord Blissford made his smile fade.

"Good evening, Dorset," said his lordship casually. He turned to Mary and beamed. "You look ravishing," he said, and bowed over her hand.

Mary blushed and murmured her thanks.

"I hope your dance card is not yet completely full."

"Nearly," said Dorset.

Lord Blissford gave Mary a teasing look. "I suppose Dorset expects you to dance every dance with him."

"Well . . ." began Mary.

"It will never do," said Lord Blissford, shaking his head. "A woman dancing every dance with her husband? It just ain't done. People will talk."

The earl was not amused. He sized up his rival. Blissford was heavier and a little taller, but he could take him in a fight. A satisfying vision of a fallen Lord Blissford with a bloodied nose and a ruined cravat came to mind and Dorset smiled.

"There," said his lordship, happily misinterpreting Dorset's smile. "Even your husband agrees. Give me this next dance and I shall be happy."

Lord Dorset listened to the violins singing in three-quarter time. "It's a waltz," he protested.

"So it is," agreed Lord Blissford. And before the earl could say anything more, he swooped Mary away like some giant evil bird.

Dorset scowled at his rival. If this was an indication of how the evening was going to go, he was not at all sure he was going to enjoy himself.

In another corner of the room Mr. Aubrey Mayhill and Miss Amanda Tuttle were carrying on an interesting conversation. "There! I have managed to save you this dance," she announced.

"I don't fell like dancing," said Aubrey. "And besides, you don't need me. There are plenty of other fools who will hop around and sweat with you."

Amanda found this a very unromantic remark and with a toss of the head informed Mr. Mayhill that she was well aware she didn't need to dance with him. "I only offered you a dance out of kindness," she said. "I could dance with any man in this room."

Aubrey took Amanda's proud statement as a challenge. "Any man?" he asked.

"Of course," she answered.

Aubrey's eyes roamed the room, resting at last

on a jaded-looking man in his forties. "How about old Newton?" he suggested. "I hear he can't abide chits just out of the schoolroom. Goes strictly for the demi-reps. Says the younger women lack conversation."

"I could make him dance with me," said Amanda confidently.

"I have five pounds says you can't," said Aubrey.

"Watch and see," she announced.

He watched as Amanda made her dainty way around the ballroom floor till she came to stand in front of Lord Newton. Aubrey's mouth dropped when the man laughed and escorted her out onto the dance floor.

Mary was not pleasantly surprised to see Amanda and Lord Newton go waltzing by. "Gracious! Whatever is she doing waltzing with Lord Newton?" she wondered aloud.

For a moment Lord Blissford allowed himself to be distracted. He eyed the other couple and shook his head. "Most unusual. Not Newton's style at all. He usually goes for older women."

"Perhaps he is interested in Amanda," said Mary.

"Perhaps," agreed his lordship noncommittally.

The dance ended and Lord Blissford reluctantly returned Mary to her husband. Lord Newton found Mary and brought Amanda to her. "I greatly enjoyed our dance, Miss Tuttle," he said, bowing. "And I hope you enjoy collecting your winnings just as much."

"Whatever did he mean by that?" asked Mary.

Before Amanda could answer, Aubrey came up. "Dang if you didn't do it!" he declared. "How did you ever get old Newton out on the floor?"

"I simply told him I stood to win five pounds if he would dance with me," said Amanda.

"No!" Aubrey was impressed.

Mary's mouth dropped. "Amanda, you didn't!"

Amanda nodded. "I certainly did. I thought it was most clever," she added in her defense. "And so did Lord Newton."

Aubrey produced the promised five pounds and Amanda put it in her beaded reticule. "Now, if you like, I shall give you a dance," she told Aubrey.

He shook his head. "I despise Scotch reels. Give me the next waltz."

At that moment Sir Percival joined them, resplendent in evening dress.

"Where the devil did you get that waistcoat?" demanded Dorset, eyeing the noxious colors.

Sir Percival ignored him. "Miss Tuttle, are you promised for this dance?"

She smiled at him. "No, and I should be

delighted to dance it with you." She turned to Aubrey. "Perhaps I shall be able to save you that waltz," she said, then allowed herself to be led away.

"If I still want it," countered Aubrey, and strolled off.

"Oh, dear," muttered Mary. "It looks very much as if they are falling in love. And Aubrey would be most unsuitable for Amanda."

"That is certain," agreed her husband. "Already his influence is unpleasantly obvious."

His wife stiffened. "I was referring to my stepbrother's lack of title and large fortune when I talked about the inappropriateness of the match."

"That, too," agreed her husband, watching Miss Tuttle and his cousin. "I should hate to see old Percy get her. He's such a nice fellow."

Unfortunately the Earl of Dorset failed to see the effect his words against her relatives were having on his wife. Her lips were pressed together tightly and the lovely bosom rose with a deep breath of indignation.

The earl shook his head. "Ah, well. It is always best to stay out of these things and let nature take its course," he said, dismissing the subject.

His wife said nothing. In fact, she said nothing the rest of the evening. Or close enough to it that her husband noticed. As they waltzed across the ballroom floor he studied her averted face. "Have I said something to offend you?" he asked.

"Whatever makes you think that?" she replied.

"You are unusually quiet," he said.

"As you have seen nothing of me these past three years, how would you know what is and is not usual for me, my lord?" she asked.

Dorset sighed. So she bore him a grudge for his past neglect. And he knew she had every right. "That is true," he conceded. "It is just that I thought we were making some progress toward being friends."

"Yes, of course," she said. "Please forgive me. That was most unkind."

"And most deserved," the earl said humbly.

She rewarded his penitence with a tiny smile and he took hope. Perhaps he would win his wife's love yet. But not before this night was over, he concluded realistically. And the thought depressed him. He watched glumly as Lord Blissford led her onto the floor for a set of country dances. She had more smiles for that rogue Blissford than she had for her own husband. Of course, Blissford had paid her more attention than her own husband had.

In the small hours of the night Lord Dorset and his party returned home. He escorted his wife to her bedroom, but all he received there was a vicious greeting from the nasty Rufus, who mangled his evening slipper and brought great pain to several toes.

He limped off to his own bed, where he lay most of the night staring at nothing and seeing a long, difficult pursuit ahead of him. He had the most beautiful woman in London for a wife, but he didn't have her heart. How did he go about winning the affections of a woman he'd ignored since he'd married her? Would he ever win the lady's love? It looked very much as if her affections were already engaged. Sadly he wondered if he were doomed to spend the rest of his life with his arms wrapped around his bed pillow instead of his wife, who lay tossing and turning in her bed next door.

-Five-

THOSE FEW WHO didn't already know of the earl's return from France soon learned of it, for the handsome young man was seen everywhere—at White's and Brooks's, on the strut in Bond Street, at the opera in the company of his lovely wife, and now, at Almack's where he stood guard over Mary, keeping all admirers at bay.

The dowager Lady Dorset joined them and shooed her son away. "Really, Jeremy. I wish you would stop hovering. It is most unnerving. Make yourself useful and fetch us some punch." Jeremy bowed and went to do his mother's bidding. She smiled at her daughter-in-law. "Does he make you feel as if you cannot breathe?" she asked.

"I must confess I am unused to receiving so much attention from my husband," said Mary.

"I daresay you are unused to receiving *any* attention from your husband," said her ladyship. "Of course, your marriage got off to an unusual start, but it couldn't last forever." Her ladyship smiled. "Men are like rats, you know. One can never quite be rid of them." She turned suddenly serious. "My dear, I hope you may not hold it against me for wishing my son home." Mary looked at her uncomprehendingly. "You must have wondered what brought him back so suddenly."

"I did wonder," admitted Mary. "But then he said he was no longer needed in France. It never occurred . . . You summoned him home?"

"No. Jeremy is long past the age where I could hope to do such a thing and meet with any success. I did write to tell him I was concerned for you. It is no small task to bring out a girl and keep track of the comings and goings of a young man enjoying his first taste of London."

"Not to mention running a gambling establishment," put in Mary. She gave her mother-in-law an accusing grin.

Her ladyship looked chagrined. "Are you very angry with me, child?"

Mary hugged the older woman. "Of course not. You have been so very kind to me since I arrived in London. I could never have managed without your guidance. And to tell the truth I am relieved to be done with my card parties. They were a great deal of work, and Jeremy has assured me we can manage quite well without the income."

"And are you managing quite well?" asked the dowager.

Mary knew her mother's old friend was not referring strictly to finances. How to answer such a question? What could she say? My husband and my brother do not get along and I feel caught in the middle . . . ? My feelings for your son are all jumbled, and to make matters worse, I find myself attracted to Lord Blissford . . . ? I am not even sure of your son's feelings for me . . . ? Heavens!

She was spared having to answer by the return of the earl himself balancing two cups of ratafia. "I suppose you two have been talking about me when I wasn't here to defend myself," he complained.

"No, you returned too soon," said his mother.

At that moment two acquaintances of his lordship's stopped to have a word with him, and his mother used it as an excuse to bear her daughter-in-law off to socialize with some other ladies. Mary stood at the edge of a little clump of women, smiling and chatting and wondering if her life would have been so complicated had she married the ever-bosky Mr. Amhearst. Out of the corner of her eye she caught sight of a handsome, blond-haired man strolling toward her.

"Good evening, Lady Dorset," said a rich voice.

"Lord Blissford," she said with a polite smile, a nod of the head, and a fluttering inside her chest.

"I suppose any number of men have already told you how lovely you look this evening. But I should be remiss in not adding my admiration to theirs."

Mary knew she should have a clever sally for this, but witty remarks had never been her strong point. And her mind was still whirling with all the unanswered questions her mother-in-law had inspired. She settled for a murmured "thank you."

"And how are you enjoying having your husband home?" asked Blissford.

"It is, naturally, very good to have him back," she said dutifully. His lordship raised a mocking eyebrow and she blushed.

"Your card parties have come to an end," he observed.

"Now that Jeremy is home, I no longer have need of them," she replied.

"Oh?" His lordship gave her a knowing look. "Almack's is more to your taste?"

Mary was unable to think of a proper answer

to his lordship's question. They both knew she preferred cards to punch, stale cake, and even staler conversation.

Dorset was bearing down on them. "I see your husband returns to guard you," said Blissford, bowing over her hand. "Good evening, fair one." He nodded a greeting to Lord Dorset and sauntered off.

His lordship watched him go and frowned. "I don't much care for that fellow, Mary. I wish you wouldn't encourage him."

Encourage him? She had done nothing to encourage him. There had been no repartee, no fan play, no fluttering lashes. How dare her husband accuse her of such a thing!

Surely he had shown no sign of such an autocratic nature when she first met him. Of course, she had known him no more than a fortnight before they were married, and then all was stiff politeness and embarrassment. How could someone learn much about another person under such burdensome circumstances?

"I want you to discourage Blissford," Dorset was saying.

Just like that. I am home now. Drop the friends you have made while I was gone. Do my bidding as though you were my servant and not my wife. . . . What difference was there, really? Mary thought angrily. Only that wives wore better clothes. "Lord Blissford was very kind to me in your absence," she began.

"Ha! I'll wager he was. And I'll wager he would like to have shown you even greater kindness, only I have returned to put a spoke in his wheel." Mary was frowning. How long had she been frowning? Lord Dorset wondered. He studied her and she turned her head, giving her attention to something on the other side of the room. The earl frowned, too. Now what the devil had he said to irritate her? Well, this would never do to be squabbling right in the middle of Almack's. He knew enough about women to realize that if he wished to return to any sort of equability, he would have to claim all responsibility for the current unpleasantness. "I am sorry I upset you," he said.

"It is only that I do not like to be made to feel like a toy soldier being fought over by two little boys," said Mary stiffly. "It was not easy making friends on my own and I am grateful to those who were so kind to me when I first arrived."

What could the earl say to such a statement? He should have been with her when she made her social debut. He should have been present to guide and encourage her. Instead he had left the task to others. If Mary had not always chosen her friends wisely, it was his fault, not hers. "I have no wish to deprive you of your friendships," he said. "I am afraid I am rather a jealous fellow and I hate to share my beautiful wife with other men."

Mary knew she should be flattered. Indeed, what woman wouldn't be if a handsome man such as Lord Dorset spoke so possessively and told her she was beautiful? She sighed. She only wished he had behaved so from the start.

Of course, she couldn't blame him really. She had been an awkward, scrawny thing with no looks when he had rescued her with his offer of marriage. She knew she had gone from an ugly duckling to a swan. And she knew she should be pleased that she had at last won her husband's admiration. But her pleasure was tarnished by the fact that he had so long neglected her.

"Tuppence for your thoughts," said Dorset.

Mary was startled out of her reverie. Her silly thoughts were nothing she could freely share with her husband. She smiled and shook her head. "They are not worth that," she said.

"Then perhaps you would care to dance?" he suggested.

Mary agreed and they headed for the dance floor. As they took their places for the quadrille she caught sight of Lord Blissford leading out Amanda and felt a twinge of unreasonable jealousy. Even though she was sure she could not love him, Mary had come to think of Lord

Blissford's admiration and attention as exclusively hers. In examining her feelings, she found she was jealous of her cousin. Amanda would have the affection of whomever she married right from the start. She would—until the novelty wore off—be petted and adored and made to feel valuable.

Mary scolded herself for her unkind and unreasonable thoughts. And besides, she told herself, your husband is making up for lost time now. Don't be such a goose. She gave him a shy smile and he beamed at her in return.

They ended the dance in charity with each other and left the dance floor smiling. Until Mary caught sight of her stepbrother. "Oh, gracious!" she gasped.

There, in a corner of the assembly room, was Aubrey, trying hard to look in control of a situation badly out of control. His face was flushed and he was speaking earnestly to a man twice his size with a face twice as red. Before he could finish speaking, the man reached out and grabbed him by the cravat, turning his complexion an even brighter color.

Dorset followed his wife's gaze. He swore under his breath. "Excuse me, my dear. I think I shall just go say hello to Aubrey."

He strode across the room, Mary following. "Evening, Hale," he greeted the large man. "You are turning my brother-in-law's face a most unflattering color."

The man let go of Aubrey with an angry shove. "The stripling owes me two hundred pounds and has been dodging me for two weeks."

"A hundred pounds a week," mused the earl as if he found the whole thing most amusing. "You fleeced him of two hundred pounds, eh?"

"Oh, no," growled the man. "That won't fly, Dorset. It was an honest game and I'll have my money."

"So you shall," said his lordship calmly. "If you would be so good as to come to me tomorrow morning at ten o'clock, I shall have the money for you."

The man nodded curtly and strode off.

"Oh, Aubrey," said Mary. "How could you?"

Aubrey looked surly. "I was going to pay him," he said. "Fact is, I could have handled him. There was no need for Dorset to come flying in and turn a rational conversation into a brawl."

Lord Dorset's jaw locked tight and his eyes narrowed.

"Aubrey," said his sister firmly. "That is a very poor way to show your gratitude to a man who has just offered to pay your debts."

"Thank you," said Aubrey. "But there was no need. I was going to pay him."

"Then you may give him the money tomorrow," said his lordship, turning to leave.

"Here now," protested Aubrey. "I can't pay him as soon as tomorrow morning. I ain't got the blunt."

"Then perhaps you had best let me take care of this debt for you," suggested his lordship.

"I thought you weren't going to bail me out," muttered Aubrey.

His lordship gave Aubrey a look that stole the flush from the youth's face, turning it to ash. "This is the last time," he said. "Next time you find yourself in dun territory I'll send you back to Lincolnshire."

By the look on his face it was plain Aubrey didn't much care for such a threat, but he wisely kept his mouth shut.

Mary was beginning to droop about twelve-thirty and the earl judged it time to bid Almack's adieu. He sent Mary in search of Amanda and went himself to fetch Aubrey. " 'Tis early yet," protested Aubrey.

"Yes, it is," agreed the earl. "But I think, perhaps, it would be best if you were to forgo your usual entertainment, as your pockets are sadly to let at the moment. Come home and I shall spot you a rubber of piquet."

Aubrey sulked but came.

Jeremy would rather have spent the remainder

of the night making love to his wife, but he instinctively knew it was too early for kisses and sweet words. Taking care of her scapegrace brother was the first step in winning his wife's heart. The look of gratitude she gave him when he bade her good night told him as much. He sighed inwardly and resigned himself to a night of callow conversation.

Aubrey wasn't a hopelessly bad cardplayer. He had some knowledge of the science of the game. But he was rash, and Jeremy could see how easily his young brother-in-law could become carried away and lose a large sum of money before he knew it. The earl studied the younger man. Aubrey was not bored, but neither was he wildly enjoying their game. "Not so exciting as hazard?" guessed the earl.

Aubrey's eyes lit up. "Now, there is a man's game."

Dorset nodded. "Plenty of excitement."

"Yes," agreed Aubrey. "Say, if you've a mind for hazard, I know of a club. . . ."

Jeremy held up a silencing hand. "Not tonight, cub." Aubrey's face fell. "Play your hand," said the earl. "There's nothing like a game of chance for emptying a man's pockets. There's nothing like a game of skill for filling them again. And your skills could use improving."

Aubrey approved of his brother-in-law's reasoning and settled down to concentrate on his hand.

Upstairs, Mary lay on her bed luxuriating in a new and cozy feeling of security.

In spite of her confused feelings for him, she was finding there were certain advantages to having her husband home. Much as she hated to admit it, she knew she could no longer control her stepbrother. It was a relief to know Jeremy would handle him—as well as everything else. She need no longer worry about running a gambling establishment, or paying for the mounting cost of Amanda's come-out. It looked very much as if her life would, at last, be worry free, if not perfect. After all, it could only be perfect if . . .

No, no! She would not entertain any foolish thoughts of happily-ever-afters or of girlhood dreams coming true. It was enough that her husband obviously no longer found her appearance a disappointment, and that he finally wanted to be friends. And anyway there was nothing so bad about simply being friends with one's husband. Heavens! Many women endured marriages with far less. With a kind husband and a pleasant cicisbeo like Lord Blissford, she could enjoy a happy, carefree life. Mary smiled and let this final happy thought escort her into a deep, dreamless sleep.

It wasn't till the following night when they

attended a ball that she began to think, perhaps, her life would not be so carefree as she'd imagined.

Lady Mumford was a voluptuous woman with thick golden curls and a pouting mouth. If she had been single, she would have been considered well past her last prayers, but as she was safely married, she found twenty-three a perfect age. She still held the blush of youth, but it sat on a body and face completely developed and ripe for dalliance. Naturally, as she was married to a much older man, her mind was as ripe as her body.

Before she spotted the Earl of Dorset, the ball had been bordering on boring. Then she saw him and her pouting mouth stretched into a smile. "Never tell me my old admirer Lord Dorset has finally returned from France," she said.

Her friend smiled wickedly. "Do not allow your hopes to rise too high, Arabella. Have you seen the wife?"

Lady Mumford dismissed the Countess of Dorset with a wave of the hand. "A chit with barely any town polish?"

"An incredibly beautiful chit," taunted her friend.

Such a taunt was not enough to destroy Lady Mumford's confidence. She smiled all the wider.

"I shall have to renew my acquaintance with his lordship."

Lady Mumford lost little time in accomplishing her goal. With a playful tap of her fan on his shoulder she gained the earl's attention and, taking a look of male admiration for encouragement, launched them into conversation.

Mary watched them from across the room with a frown on her face.

"I see your husband and Lady Mumford are becoming reacquainted," said a plain woman Mary had recently met. "The earl was quite fond of her at one time. Of course, they could never make a match of it. She had to marry money. And he . . ." The woman caught herself. "And he, of course, met you."

Mary knew what her informant had been about to say. "And he had to marry money as well." She smiled and changed the subject, but out of the corner of her eye she continued to regard the woman with whom her husband chatted so amiably. She noted the lady's clinging gown, cut so low her breasts threatened to pop out of it, the pouting mouth, the clever way she leaned close to Jeremy when she talked, as if tempting him to touch her.

Mary's companion finally tired of tormenting her and left her to size up her competition in peace. Lady Mumford was a beautiful woman.

There was no denying it. And if her husband wished to talk with a beautiful woman, who was she to object? Her marriage to Jeremy had been based on kindness, not love. And even if it had been based on love, she could hardly object every time he talked with a lovely lady.

"She's a fine-looking woman, in a bawdy sort of way," said a new voice at Mary's elbow.

She turned to see Lord Blissford and blushed, embarrassed that he had so obviously read her thoughts.

"I prefer a little more subtlety in a beautiful woman," he said.

"I think, perhaps, you are an exceptional man," said Mary wistfully.

"Do you?" teased his lordship. "How fortunate for me. You are looking absolutely delicious tonight, my dear," he said. He took her hand and turned it palm up. He regarded it as if it were, indeed, a delicacy before bringing it to his mouth. He kissed her wrist with a slow, savoring kiss during which she felt the tickle of his tongue.

She bit her lip, feeling guilty for the little thrill he sent through her.

"As your husband is occupied, perhaps I can induce you to dance with me," he said.

Mary looked across the room. Jeremy was, indeed, still talking with Lady Mumford, who now had her arm linked with his and was leading him to two empty chairs along the wall. Mary smiled up at her companion. "I should love to dance," she said. And determined not to let her husband's lack of allegiance affect her life in the least, she flashed Lord Blissford a dazzling smile.

As they waltzed out onto the floor he said, "I should not let your husband's friendship with Lady Mumford upset me if I were you."

"It does not in the least," said Mary lightly.

His lordship smiled down at her. "Good. For I can assure you that such friendships are very much the way of things. Few husbands appreciate their wives. It is natural for a married woman to seek admiration elsewhere."

"And my husband is Lady Mumford's elsewhere?" guessed Mary.

"Perhaps," said his lordship. "And, perhaps, your husband does not properly appreciate you." Mary bit her lip. "Never mind," he continued. "You have an entire horde of admirers, and I am at the head of it."

What was Lord Blissford trying to tell her? No use pretending she didn't know. Mary blushed. "Thank you," she said.

The dance ended. "You look warm," he told her. "Perhaps a little fresh air?" Before Mary could object, he led her out a set of French doors, which seemed to have magically appeared, and onto a small balcony.

Nervously she leaned against the railing, her back to her companion. " 'Tis a lovely night," she observed. "And unseasonably warm."

She felt two hands on her arms and shivered. "Your husband is a fool," said Lord Blissford. He placed a kiss on her shoulder and her heart began to thump against her chest as if beating to be let out. His lordship kissed the base of her neck.

Now she was shaking somewhere deep inside her limbs. She bit her lower lip to keep her teeth from chattering. His lordship nibbled her earlobe and she shivered violently. "We had best go in," she said. "I am afraid I am very cold."

"I suspect, my dear, you are quite the opposite," whispered Blissford.

Mary pretended not to have heard this comment, preceding him back into the ballroom.

He followed her, a smile teasing the corners of his mouth.

Once back inside the ballroom they encountered Lord Dorset. "Mary! I've been looking for you this past half hour," he said.

Blissford cocked an eyebrow as if to say, *Was Lady Mumford assisting you?*

Lord Dorset ignored him. "I have not seen Miss Tuttle in some time," he said.

"Oh, dear," fretted Mary. "I hope she has not gotten into mischief."

"Knowing your protégée, I should guess that is exactly what she has gotten into," said her husband. "Perhaps we should look for her. I am sure Lord Blissford will excuse us." With that he hurried his wife away.

Mary scanned the corners of the ballroom with nervous eyes. Wherever could Amanda be? What disturbing new event lurked in the shadows to further turn her life upside down? They passed a cluster of potted palms and she caught sight of a blue flounce protruding from behind a jardiniere. Peeking around the foliage, she was just in time to see Amanda leaning toward Aubrey, her lips puckered. "Amanda!" she gasped.

Both Amanda and Aubrey jumped and turned matching red faces toward her. "Mary," said her stepbrother.

"There is no need to ask what you are doing," said Dorset. "One might ask why?"

"I am paying my debt," announced Amanda. "I lost a wager with Aubrey and I owed him a kiss."

Mary gave Aubrey a disapproving look. "I am afraid this is one debt you shan't be able to pay," she said to the girl, and, taking her arm, led her away. "I think, perhaps, it is time we left."

"But the ball is not over," protested Amanda.

"It is for us," said Mary firmly. "My head is aching something fierce. We shall have to go home." And as they waited for their carriage to be brought 'round, she realized the jagged pounding behind her eyes stemmed not from her charge's fast behavior, but from the realization that her assumption of the previous night had been erroneous. Her husband's return had not made her life worry free in the least.

-*Six*-

SIR PERCIVAL CALLED the following morning, offering to take Miss Tuttle for a drive in his curricle. "See the spring flowers and that sort of thing," he explained.

After the previous night Mary was only too happy to be free of her troublesome charge for a while and sent them off with her blessing.

They had barely gotten down the street when Miss Tuttle questioned him on the importance of paying one's debts.

"A fellow should always pay his gambling debts," said Sir Percy.

"And a lady?" prompted Amanda.

"A gambling debt is a debt of honor, no matter who incurs it," he replied.

"I thought so," said Amanda, satisfied.

Sir Percy regarded her suspiciously. "Have you a gambling debt to pay?"

Amanda nodded. "And my cousin Mary is none too happy about it."

"Can you pay it? That is, if you are in need of assistance . . . " Percy began.

Amanda met his gallant offer with a giggle. "I am well able to pay it on my own, I assure you," she said, and changed the subject, leaving Sir Percival to wonder what sort of trouble the beautiful Miss Tuttle was into and whether he should tell Jeremy or try to help her himself.

Mary had had no qualms about sending Amanda off in Percy's company. She knew Percy at least would not be making ridiculous wagers with the child and encouraging her in fast behavior. Amanda would be pleasantly entertained for the morning and Mary could relax.

But relaxation was not in the cards for Lady Dorset. No sooner had she dispatched Amanda than her mother-in-law sent up her card. Mary was not feeling up to seeing anyone, even the dowager countess, but one could hardly send away one's own mother-in-law. Her ladyship was shown up to Mary's sitting room.

Mary donned what she was sure must be a cheerful smile. "You are out and about early," she said.

The dowager took Mary's chin in her hand and studied her face. "Are you finding the London season more wearing than you anticipated?"

"It is all a little overwhelming," said Mary.

"And I am afraid," said her ladyship, "the nobility does not always behave nobly, which makes it all the more wearing."

Mary bit her lip. Her mother-in-law had been at the ball. It would have been truly remarkable if she hadn't seen her son with Lady Mumford. And had she seen his wife slip onto the balcony in the company of Lord Blissford? Mary felt a guilty blush blooming on her face.

"Lady Mumford is and always was a conceited creature of questionable morals," said her ladyship. "I was not sorry when she made her come-out to learn she was after bigger fish than my son. But she led him a merry dance before making her choice."

"Was her husband at the ball last night?" asked Mary.

Her ladyship nodded. "Oh, yes. He was the old fool beaming on the side of the dance floor while his wife amused herself with a score of other men."

Mary remembered seeing Lady Mumford sitting next to a rheumy-eyed man with a gold-headed cane. But surely he couldn't be Lord Mumford. He was so very old. "The man with the cane?" she asked.

Her ladyship nodded. "That is the one. He is disgusting, is he not? Arabella has made her bed, but she rarely lies in it. Not with her lord, at any rate." Mary sighed and her mother-in-law patted her arm. "Never mind, love. She is no threat to you."

Mary smiled at her. "Is that why you called, to assure me of my husband's undying devotion?"

The dowager's eyes opened in a good imitation of surprise. "Why, now that you mention it, I suppose it is!" she declared.

The butler came in with a large silver tray complete with tea service and a plate of tiny cakes. "Now that your mission is accomplished, I hope you will stay and drink a dish of tea," said Mary.

The tea had barely been poured when the subject of their earlier conversation put his head in at the door. "Mother! What are you doing here?"

"I am drinking tea," said his mother.

"Will you join us?" offered his wife.

His lordship consented and spent the next twenty minutes with the ladies. At the end of this time his mother set down her cup and announced her need to be on her way. "I simply must find a new bonnet. And I have a fitting with Madame Levaine at one."

"I shall see you out," offered her son. "Now," he said as he walked his mother to her carriage, "why were you really here?"

She turned wide eyes to him. "Why, to pay a morning call on Mary. Can a woman not call on her daughter-in-law without arousing suspicion?"

"Not mine," said the earl. "You are usually much too busy calling on your friends to bother with your son."

"But I was not bothering with my son," protested her ladyship. "I was calling on my daughter."

"It is not like you to meddle, Mother. So confess. What worries you now?"

"Lady Mumford," replied her ladyship. "She tires of her current lover and looks for new amusement. It would amuse her greatly to lure you away from your beautiful wife."

"I am sure it would," agreed Dorset. He cocked his head. "Do you think it possible?"

"I think it possible for two people to keep their thoughts to themselves and drift into misunderstanding," said her ladyship.

"I shall not let us drift. Never fear," said the earl. "It was good to see you, Mother." With that pleasant farewell the earl handed his mother into her carriage. He watched it drive off and hoped he would be able to do as he'd said.

There was no time that morning for the earl to attempt to anchor his marriage, for he had no sooner watched his mother's carriage drive off than Sir Percival's curricle drove up, returning Miss Tuttle. The earl sighed inwardly. He knew now that Miss Tuttle was returned, the rest of the day would be consumed with shopping and dress fittings. Promising to meet Sir Percival later at White's, he retired to the library, ostensibly to work, in reality to think how he could best rid himself of Lady Mumford's attention and win his wife's lasting affection.

His vagabond existence in France had made dalliance an easy matter. His experiences with French trollops had made handling women seem deceptively easy. The earl was fast learning that flirting with a pretty woman or bedding a willing tavern maid was much different than trying to win a beautiful wife who was being wooed by another man, especially while fending off the unwanted attentions of a demi-rep at the same time.

It should be simple. He should simply be able to say to Mary, "Look here, my dear. I was a fool ever to leave you and I will never do so again. I have no desire to become entangled with Arabella Mumford or any other woman. The only woman I want is you, always and forever."

Mary would reply, "Oh, Jeremy," and run into his arms. . . . No, blast it. She would gaze at him with that shy, wounded look and murmur her thanks and he would feel foolish and awkward. . . . No! If she gives me that look, I shall grab her and pull her into my arms and kiss her till she's breathless. . . . And that curst pug of hers will rush my feet. And I shall boot it out and lock the boudoir door! he finished triumphantly. He would win not only his wife's affections but her respect as well, and he would do so before the season was over. And nothing would stop him!

Feeling triumphant and invincible, the Earl of Dorset left for his club to celebrate his sunny future.

He passed the dandies in White's bow window, his eyes searching for his cousin. As luck would have it, Sir Percival was coming his way. He smiled and clapped his cousin on the back. "Well, old fellow. I see you are making progress with the fair Miss Tuttle."

Sir Percy shook his head. "Don't think she even considers me an admirer, let alone a suitor. Has she been . . . Oh, never mind."

"What is it, Percy?" prompted his lordship.

Sir Percy hesitated. "Don't know if I should tell you."

"Tell me what?" demanded Dorset.

"She was asking me about paying one's debts this morning. Said something about a wager."

Jeremy frowned. "Foolish chit. She was probably referring to some foolish wager she'd made with Aubrey. She was about to forfeit a kiss when we caught them behind a potted palm at the ball last night."

Sir Percival's eyes widened. "Good Lord," he said.

The earl nodded. "She bids well to be a handful for whoever marries her," he said. "You weren't leaving, were you?"

"No, no. Knew you were coming," said Sir Percy. "I was just having a look to see whether you'd arrived." He cleared his throat nervously as the two men settled themselves at a small table. "Speaking of wagers, there's been some serious betting going on here today."

A liveried servant produced a tray with a pack of cards and Jeremy casually took them and began to shuffle. "Oh?" he said, trying to sound casual. "Regarding what?"

"*Whom* is more like it," said Sir Percy. "And the whom is you."

The earl grimaced. "And what are they wagering about me?"

"Whether you'll have the Mumford or no."

Jeremy frowned. "Who started this? Do you know?"

Sir Percy shook his head. "Can't be sure, but I saw Blissford in the thick of it."

Jeremy chewed his lip as he dealt out the cards. "If this should get back to Mary, I'll have the devil's own time winning her over," he predicted.

"Let's hope it don't," said Sir Percy.

But is was Sir Percy himself who spilled the news. At the next ball the earl and his wife attended Lady Mumford begged to be introduced to the countess. "I have been admiring you from a distance these past two balls," she complained. "Lord Dorset has been most slack in fulfilling his social obligations. And how are you enjoying London? I understand it is your first season with us."

She smiled politely at Mary, all courteous attention, wishing to know from what backwater the young countess hailed that it had taken her so long to become part of the ton.

"It *is* my first season," confessed Mary. "And I am enjoying it very much."

Her ladyship's attention had begun to wander before Mary could even finish her reply. Now she cocked her head, listening to the music. "A waltz!" she declared. "I adore the waltz. Lord Dorset, you simply must waltz with me." She beamed graciously at Mary. "It is so tedious to dance with one's own husband, is it not? I shall rescue you just this once."

Mary watched, stupefied, as Lady Mumford glided off with her husband.

Sir Percy, who had been present to witness the theft, scratched his head. "No wonder the odds were on Mumford," he muttered.

"Odds?" repeated Mary. "What odds?"

Sir Percy tried to feign ignorance. "What?" he asked, leaning an ear toward Mary as if he'd suddenly turned deaf.

"You heard me," she said. "Is there some sort of wager floating 'round about my husband and Lady Mumford?"

"Well . . . that is . . ." began Sir Percy.

"Never mind," said Mary. Sadly she watched Lady Mumford smile up into her husband's face. "Percy, perhaps you would care to fetch me some punch." There was a catch in her voice and she cursed herself for betraying her emotions. Sir

86

Percy opened his mouth to speak. "Please," she said. "I am very thirsty."

He gave up and left her.

Oh, dear, Mary thought. She was going to cry. The dam had broken and she couldn't hold back the tears any longer. With hurried steps she made her way to the door.

Strong arms caught her before she could make her escape. "Here now," said Lord Blissford. "What has happened to upset you?"

"Nothing," stammered Mary. "I am not feeling well. That is all."

His lordship studied her averted face. "And I can guess what hurts," he said.

"Oh, please let me go," pleaded Mary.

"And waste a perfectly good waltz?" Lord Blissford put his hand on her waist and pulled her out onto the floor. "You must not let your husband's friendship distress you so," he counseled. "A mild flirtation now and again means nothing. We all change partners frequently. It is the way of things."

Change partners? I have yet to *be* my husband's partner, Mary thought sadly. "I am sure my husband may dance with whomever he pleases," she said, trying to sound like a woman of the world.

"And so may you," said his lordship.

Mary suddenly found herself uncomfortably aware of the hard, muscled shoulder beneath the cloth of her partner's evening coat. She gave herself a mental shake. What mad temptation was this? Where were her thoughts straying? It would never do to console herself in the arms of Lord Blissford. Charming as he was, she was sure he was a rake. And she strongly suspected if she were to encourage his attentions, she would lose all hope of ever gaining the perfect marriage she had once dreamed of.

But how to even get her husband's attention? And how to get him out of the clutches of Lady Mumford? Mary found herself wishing she had not led quite such a secluded life. If only she'd had her London season. She felt sure she'd have known how to get on better. You will simply have to learn, my girl, she told herself. And soon.

Sir Percy found her as soon as the dance was ended and presented her with her punch. Lady Mumford returned her husband to her and Lord Blissford beat a dignified retreat. If only they would all leave us alone, thought Mary. Perhaps then we would have a chance.

On the way home from the ball Miss Tuttle was full of lively chatter. "Of course, the ball was not half so much fun without Aubrey. He would be well served if I were to encourage Mr. Whiting. I hear he is rich as Croesus. I think he is becoming very much interested in me. Mr. Whiting, that is."

Lost in her own painful thoughts, Mary let Amanda's prattle wash over her. But one name lodged painfully against her heart, forcing her to give Amanda her attention.

"Lady Mumford is exceeding handsome, is she not?" Amanda was saying. "I wish my gowns were half so fine as hers."

Lady Mumford! She even follows me home, thought Mary irritably. "You may console yourself with the knowledge that her gowns are not even half so modest as yours," she said.

"Mary is right," said Dorset. "Neither Lady Mumford's gowns nor her behavior are any proper model for a young lady."

"Do you not find her beautiful, then?" asked Amanda.

During his years abroad Lord Dorset had been a clever spy. He had employed the smoothest of tongues when necessary and glibly lied, but here in their carriage, with his wife regarding him intently, he found himself tongue-tied. "Well, er . . . Of course she's beautiful, but that don't signify."

Amanda looked perplexed.

"What Jeremy is trying to say," put in Mary, "is that there is more to a woman than her looks."

The earl looked relieved. "Yes. That is what I was trying to say," he said.

And does he really believe that? wondered Mary. If he does, he has changed much since he left his bride for the continent three years ago.

Her maid was brushing out her hair when his lordship knocked on her door. She bit her lip, wishing it would be enough to calm her dancing heart. "Come in," she called.

The earl entered and the abigail slipped away. He looked at his wife. The candlelight caught the red in her hair, making it glow with a warmth he was sure he could feel if he touched it. She didn't turn to look at him, but sat staring at her looking glass, her back straight, the soft curves of her body outlined in some gossamer material. She looked like an actress in a play, waiting to say her lines. The earl swallowed. Once again he felt at a loss for words.

His wife broke the silence. "Did you mean what you said tonight? In the carriage?"

"I did," he replied. He came to stand in back of her and twined a strand of hair around his finger. Lovely, soft stuff. It smelled of flowers.

"Mary. About Lady Mumford . . . " There was a rap on the bedroom door. His lordship frowned and opened it.

There stood the butler, his face apologetic. "I am sorry to disturb your lordship, but it would appear Mr. Mayhill has been hurt."

– Seven –

"AUBREY!" GASPED MARY. Her husband was already out the door and she followed him down the stairs. Halfway down they encountered the victim himself. With a footman on each side, he was being half dragged, half carried. Mary pressed a hand to her mouth to control the wild, fearful sobbing swelling in her chest. The earl turned and followed them upstairs to Aubrey's bedroom and she trailed behind like a forlorn ghost.

Dorset gave orders as the men laid Aubrey on his bed. "John, fetch the doctor. Gregory, bring me warm water and some torn sheets. And tell Jeffries to bring up some brandy." He then set to work removing Aubrey's jacket. The younger man gasped from the pain. "Well, cub. And how did you come to get this?" asked Dorset casually.

"Not my fault," panted Aubrey. "The hazard table was unfair."

"So you were at seventy-seven Jermyn Street, eh?"

Aubrey grimaced and swore under his brother-in-law's ministrations, mumbling oaths. "Curse it, Dorset. You've got hands like an ox."

"Just wait till the sawbones gets here," said the earl, unmoved. "He'll put you through twice as much. The ball is lodged in your shoulder. It will have to be dug out." At that moment the butler appeared with a bottle of brandy and a glass. His lordship ignored the glass, handing the bottle to Aubrey. "Drink up," he commanded.

The footman reappeared with water and sheets. A pale-faced Mary took it from him and brought it to her husband. "Why don't you wait downstairs?" he suggested. "This is not a pretty sight."

She shook her head. "I shall help you," she said.

The doctor arrived within the hour and sent both the earl and his wife away. They went down to the drawing room. The fire had long since burned out and the room was cold. Mary shivered under her wrapper and took a seat near the hearth.

The earl grabbed some pieces of wood and quickly brought the fire back to life. He leaned on the mantelpiece and rubbed his gritty eyes, silently cursing the foolish youth for his poor timing. Really, he was a spoiled thing.

"Will he be all right?" asked Mary.

"Lord, yes," said the earl wearily. "He'll come out of this little worse for the wear. If anything, it will teach him a lesson." Dorset shook his head. "He's been too much indulged. A little suffering is just what he needs."

Mary stiffened. Already tired and upset by Lady Mumford's brazen manipulation of her husband, she found his criticism of her stepbrother was the final straw. She pressed her lips tightly together in an effort not to cry. How could Jeremy criticize her so heartlessly? She had tried the best she could to be like a parent to Aubrey. But an older sister wasn't the same as a father. What he had needed was a man's guidance. If her husband had been present to offer Aubrey a firm hand in the first place, this would probably never have happened. If he had stayed with her instead of running away. Mary found herself suddenly feeling very cool toward her husband.

After half an hour the doctor was shown into the drawing room. He announced the success of his operation and predicted a speedy recovery for his patient. "I suppose he'll have an awful head in the morning to go with his pained shoulder." The little man shook his head. "It was really very foolish to give him an entire bottle of brandy. I have the most difficult time convincing my patients that it is a most unwise practice.''

Mary shot an angry glance at her husband, who merely shrugged off the doctor's words.

"Give him some laudanum for the pain. Keep him abed the rest of the week," he said crisply, and left the earl and his countess.

The earl studied his wife. She would not meet his eyes, but sat looking at the fire with great determination, making it clear that somehow he had managed to say or do the wrong thing. He thought wistfully of that moment in her bedroom, which had trembled with promise, and cursed his rotten luck.

Well, this was not the time to woo her. She was too upset over that scapegrace brother of hers. And too tired. "You look fagged to death," he said. "Why don't you go get some rest."

"I should sit with Aubrey," she said.

"There is nothing you can do tonight. Your brother would be better served by you securing a good night's rest, for I'll warrant he will not be an easy patient. You will have your hands full keeping him entertained the next few days." Mary still hesitated. "Go on now," said the earl, taking her gently by the arm and leading her to the door. "You are dead on your feet."

Mary didn't argue further. She was, indeed,

exhausted. She would have to deal with the men in her life tomorrow. For what was left of tonight she must sleep.

And sleep she did. So soundly that she was completely unaware of the handsome figure who stood beside her bed and smiled tenderly at her. She barely stirred when he tucked the blankets that had fallen from her shoulder up under her chin and dropped a kiss on her forehead.

Amanda was all agog the next morning, dying for details of Aubrey's adventure and upset that she had managed to sleep through the entire thing. "How did he come to get shot?" she asked.

"He got into an argument with some fellow in a gaming hell," said the earl casually. "But it is only a shoulder wound and he should mend quickly," he finished. He tried to send his wife an encouraging smile, but she appeared preoccupied with removing the shell from a boiled egg.

"How simply terrible," said Amanda. "Is he in great pain? May I see him?"

"I think, perhaps, we had best let him rest today," said Mary.

Amanda looked disappointed. She fell silent a moment. But only for a moment. "He is quite all right, though?" she asked, seeking reassurance.

"He will be up and around in a matter of days, and probably squiring you to balls within a fortnight," said the earl.

"Poor Aubrey," Amanda sighed and turned to Mary. "What shall we do today? Should we, perhaps, have some flowers sent 'round to cheer him up, or something from Gunther's?"

The earl excused himself and left the ladies making plans to lift the spirits of the invalid. "It is as if he were wounded in battle," he complained to his cousin, who called later that day.

Sir Percy shook his head. "I got in a fight in a hell once. My father said it served me right and paid the doctor's bill out of my quarter's allowance."

At that moment Miss Tuttle entered the drawing room. "Oh, Sir Percy! Have you heard the news about Aubrey? Is it not dreadful? Why, he could have been killed!"

Sir Percy nodded his agreement then produced a posy for Amanda. "Here's a little something," he said.

She smiled up at him. "How sweet," she said. "Just what Aubrey needs to cheer him. I shall take it to Mary straightaway."

She left before Sir Percy could stop her. He shrugged helplessly at his cousin, who was trying hard not to laugh.

"I don't know, old fellow," said Dorset. "You

must be the most star-crossed lover I ever encountered." He then thought of himself. "Or nearly the most," he amended, the smile falling from his face.

The following day Aubrey professed himself well enough to sit in the drawing room by the fire. "I had enough of laying in bed yesterday," he said. "Besides, only my shoulder hurts. The rest of me is fine."

His sister relented. He emerged from the sickroom the picture of health. Only the scarlet dressing gown worn over his shirt and pantaloons hinted at a possible wound. So far that morning he had sent servants scurrying for everything imaginable, from an extra pillow for his back to more marmalade for his muffin. He had been restless and fidgety, and in only an hour his sister had tried three different card games to amuse him. Perhaps Amanda could keep him entertained, she thought hopefully.

Amanda was impressed when she found him in the drawing room. "How do you feel today? Does it hurt terribly?" She reached out a hand as if to touch the wound, then, recovering herself, hurried to plump up the sofa cushions for him.

"It hurts like the very devil," said Aubrey, "but I feel better than I did yesterday."

"Is there anything I can get you, dearest?" asked Mary.

"Perhaps a glass of sherry," suggested the invalid.

Mary fetched him a small glass. "I must confer with Cook about dinner," she said. "I shall be back to check on you directly. Meanwhile perhaps Amanda will keep you company."

"Oh, yes," agreed Amanda eagerly. "I have been wanting to hear all the details, but you were in no condition to talk yesterday, and no one has told me much of anything. In fact," she said, watching her cousin's retreating back and lowering her voice, "no one seems to be properly upset by your misfortune at all."

Aubrey made a face. "Dorset don't care. He thinks I brought it on myself, most like. As if I would go out and try to get myself shot," Aubrey concluded scornfully. "I was just trying to make things right, protect the poor flats who were being gulled. The house runs a crooked hazard table. I suspected as much. Finally caught 'em at it. And they didn't take any too kindly to having me come in and ferret out their little secret, I can tell you."

"Gracious," breathed Amanda. "Was that when you got shot?"

Aubrey nodded importantly. "Made a big ruckus. I taught those sharps a thing or two. Till I got shot," he finished. He tried to move his shoulder and winced.

"Oh, dear!" Amanda jumped up and readjusted the sofa pillow behind him. "You poor, brave man."

Fortunately for Aubrey's self-importance Lord Dorset was not present to laugh at this tender scene. The earl had decided that perhaps he was not so capable of straightening out his romantic affairs as he had thought and was, at the moment, en route to pay a morning call on his mother. He really wasn't sure what she could do, but he had some hazy idea of seeing if she might not have a word with Mary, discover what he had now done to offend his wife.

Once ensconced in the sofa in her drawing room, however, he found himself unable to broach the subject.

The dowager regarded him from over her teacup. "How is your sherry, dear?" she asked.

"Quite tolerable," he replied, downing it.

"Now that you have fortified yourself, perhaps you might tell me why you called," suggested her ladyship. "I hear Aubrey has gotten himself shot."

"'Tis nothing serious," said Dorset.

"Only to his sister," said his mother agreeably.

The earl frowned. "I should send him packing. And the Tuttle chit, too."

Her ladyship grinned. "Are you finding it

difficult to court your wife with so many people in the house?'' she teased.

''I am finding it curst difficult to court my wife with or without people,'' snapped the earl. ''I cannot understand her, Mother.''

''And so you come to me?'' Her son fidgeted. ''Ah, no,'' she said. ''I am done meddling. If you want Mary, you must win her. And that will not be easy.''

''It has already proven difficult,'' said the earl crossly.

Her ladyship showed little inclination toward sympathy. ''Every knight must fight his dragon, my son. And yours is your past behavior. It will not be easy to banish the memory of your indifference from your wife's mind. But there is nothing I or anyone else can really do to help you. You must face this particular dragon alone.''

His mother was right, the earl thought despondently as he made his way home. No one could help him. And winning Mary's affections was a doubly difficult task with so many people milling about trying to hinder him. There was Blissford, dancing 'round Mary with that devilish grin and that equally devilish mind. Jeremy knew Blissford would take great delight in cuckolding him and figure he had it coming for leaving her in the first place. He had to win

Mary's affections before Blissford swept her completely off her feet.

Then there was Aubrey. What to do about the cub? He was definitely a source of irritation. The earl drummed his fingers on his leg as his carriage made its way through the streets of Mayfair. Suddenly, like a gift from heaven, an idea came to him. Ha! he thought. It would be the perfect thing for the boy and the perfect way to remove him from underfoot. It was positively inspired! The earl promised himself he would start working on that particular idea first thing the following morning.

Once Aubrey was disposed of, all he would be left with was Miss Tuttle. Miss Tuttle. There was a curst nuisance if ever he'd seen one. It was she who had been the reason for his wife's setting up a gambling establishment. And it was she who took so much of Mary's time. But if Miss Tuttle were to secure herself a husband, she could be shipped home to start making wedding plans.

The earl bit his lip gleefully. Surely there must be some poor fool anxious to marry the chit. She hadn't much fortune, but maybe he could throw in a little something to sweeten the pot and hurry the whole process. And if he were to succeed in getting Miss Tuttle engaged, he would be doing old Percy a favor, too. After all, Percy was a good fellow. He deserved better than a girl who backed into trouble every time she turned around. Yes, he would attend to Miss Tuttle's future the next week at Almack's.

The earl smiled, seeing himself victorious, his foot resting on a heap of slain dragons.

-Eight-

AUBREY'S RECOVERY WAS, as the doctor had predicted, a speedy one. The first two or three days he had tired quickly, but as the week progressed he became increasingly stronger. And increasingly more restless. Finally he reached a point where he swore that even the thought of an evening spent at dull old Almack's, where the refreshments were inferior, the card play insipid, and the dance floor poor, looked like a treat. And as the earl had his own reasons for wanting to visit dull old Almack's, the family attended.

Once through those sacred portals, Lord Dorset wasted no time. "Well," he declared when they were barely inside the ballroom. "Here comes Lord Barnhill." He hailed a beefy middle-aged man. "You are looking fit tonight, your lordship."

Mary eyed Lord Barnhill's bulging paunch and wondered, Fit for what?

"I believe you have met my wife. Allow me to present her cousin Miss Amanda Tuttle, who is staying with us."

Miss Tuttle dropped his lordship a curtsy and he looked at her as though she were a tasty morsel.

"I am sure Miss Tuttle would like to start her evening off with a dance," suggested Dorset.

Before she quite knew what had happened, Miss Tuttle found herself being led away from her party by the hungry-looking Lord Barnhill.

"I wish you hadn't done that," protested Aubrey. "I was going to ask Amanda to dance."

"You can hardly dance in your condition," said his lordship. "It would only reopen your wound. And you wouldn't wish to bleed all over your coat, would you?"

Aubrey scowled and stalked off.

"Must you tease him?" asked Mary unhappily.

His lordship was instantly penitent. "I am sorry," he said.

"Would he really reopen his wound?"

"Most likely," said his lordship. "He should have a care." Sir Percival joined them and Dorset eyed his waistcoat. "Now, if ever there was a waistcoat that deserved to be bled upon, here it is. You could take a lesson in dress from your rival, old fellow. Have you seen Aubrey's? Pale blue. Inoffensive to the eye. And only one fob."

Sir Percy looked down at the brightly flowered creation showing beneath his evening coat. "I rather like it," he said.

His lordship merely shook his head. "I quite lose hope," he said. He turned to his wife. "Would you care for some punch?"

Mary nodded and he left them. On his way to the punch bowl she noticed he stopped to converse with a man in his late fifties who was nearly as hefty as Lord Barnhill. But where Lord Barnhill's face was florid, this man's face was pasty. He looked like a gigantic lump of dough waiting to be kneaded. "To whom is Jeremy speaking?" she asked Sir Percy.

Sir Percival squinted across the room. "Norton," he said. "Fellow has fifty thousand pounds a year to his credit, and word has it he is hanging out for a young wife. His first wife died three years ago."

Sir Percy was hailed by a friend, and while he and the other man talked Mary studied her husband's progress toward the punch bowl. Two other men were stopped with a hearty clap on the back. Once she saw her husband nodding toward the dance floor. How very curious, she thought.

Aubrey joined her. "What the devil is Dorset up to?" he demanded. "I just overheard him talking to old Norton, puffing off Miss Tuttle as though she were a countess."

Sir Percy continued nodding politely to his friend and craned his head in Aubrey's direction.

"It does seem rather odd that he should take such a sudden interest in Amanda's future," mused Mary. "But I suppose I can hardly object to his wishing to help her make a good match."

Sir Percy frowned.

"A good match!" echoed Aubrey. "With that old curmudgeon? He'd hardly do for Miss Tuttle. She needs someone young, someone who can keep pace with her." Mary raised a curious eyebrow and her brother blushed. "It ain't right to even think of marrying a girl like Miss Tuttle to such an old goat," he said. "I'm going to dance the next dance with her myself."

"But your shoulder," began Mary.

"The devil take my shoulder," snapped Aubrey.

"Aubrey, don't be foolish," she protested. But it was too late. Her brother was already crossing the floor in search of Amanda.

Aubrey needn't have worried about Miss Tuttle falling into the hands of an old goat such as Lord Norton, for Dorset was talking with the younger men as well. In fact, he was singing Miss Tuttle's praises to nearly every available male in the room.

At the punch bowl Dorset encountered Sir Percy, who informed him he was fetching the punch his lordship had promised his wife half an hour ago. "I suppose you've been too busy trying to fire off Miss Tuttle." Sir Percy looked at his cousin, the traitor, accusingly.

"Now, Percy. Don't get your feathers ruffled. 'Tis nothing personal. But I have to get Amanda safely engaged and out of my life. If you want the chit, you'd best hurry up and make a push for her, for I mean to be rid of her as soon as possible."

Sir Percy set his mouth in determination. He handed his cousin the cup of punch and strode across the room just in time to see Aubrey step in front of Miss Tuttle. She smiled up at him and allowed him to lead her out onto the dance floor for a waltz. Sir Percy frowned and consoled himself by going to speak with a sweet, brown-haired girl whose conversation he'd enjoyed the previous night at a dinner party.

"Is this going to hurt your shoulder?" asked Amanda in concern.

"Never mind my shoulder," said Aubrey.

"Did you know Dorset is trying to pop you off to old Norton?"

Amanda's face paled. "Lord Norton? The fat man with the clammy hands?"

"That's the one," said Aubrey, nodding. "You'd best be careful not to give him any encouragement or you'll find yourself engaged before the cat can lick its ear."

"You must not let him near me," pleaded Amanda.

"Never fear," said Aubrey. "I shan't let that old fool get you."

Lord Dorset watched the young couple dancing and frowned. If ever there was a match made in hell, it had to be Miss Tuttle and the cub. Aubrey was barely dry behind the ears. And Miss Tuttle was a hen-witted little fool who promised to spend the next few years falling in and out of more scrapes than the earl cared to witness. He hoped one of the poor fools he'd talked to offered for her soon. Miss Tuttle needed to be wed, bred, and locked away in the country before she caused serious trouble.

"Oh! For me? How ever did you know I was dying of thirst?"

His lordship turned to see Lady Mumford smiling beside him. Another dragon to slay. He gave up the punch cup and she sipped from it, regarding him over the rim.

On the other side of the room Mary watched sadly. Her husband was so busy tonight, talking with everyone but her. Not for the first time she told herself she'd been a fool to marry the earl. He had been so handsome, so kind, the quintessential hero. She had adored him. He had left her. Now he was home, but still he was not with her. Because she was not lovely enough to suit him? That smile he had just given Lady Mumford, had it been merely polite? Mary could have sworn she'd seen his eyes light up.

Lord Blissford stopped to bid her good evening. "I can hardly credit my good fortune—finding you alone with no swarm of admirers, no group of ladies."

Mary merely smiled and returned her gaze to the far corner of the room.

"Would you care to make a wager?" asked Blissford. "I shall wager my new snuffbox against your fan that she has him on the floor within five minutes."

Mary gave his lordship a crippled smile. "The odds are against me, but I shall take it." She tried to make her voice light.

"Good girl," said Blissford encouragingly.

Much to Mary's surprise they had barely made

their wager when her husband bowed to Lady Mumford and left her gaping by the punch bowl.

Mary flashed a triumphant smile at Lord Blissford and held out her hand.

With a sardonic smile he pulled out an enameled snuffbox and laid it in her palm.

Lord Dorset searched the crowd, and when he caught sight of his wife and Lord Blissford, a determined look settled on his face. He made his way around the edge of the room, stopping only to haul his cousin away from the brow-haired girl, coming to a stop in front of Mary and Lord Blissford.

"Good evening, Blissford," he said casually. He turned to his wife. "Would you care for some ratafia, my dear?"

"You asked her that over an hour ago," muttered Percy.

"Yes, I would," answered Mary politely.

"Fine," said Dorset. "Here, Percy. Be a good fellow and take Mary and get her some punch."

Percy looked confused, but he offered Mary his arm and led her away.

Lord Dorset gave his rival a cool smile. "You have been most attentive to my wife," he observed. "And I am sure she was glad of a friend in my absence."

"But I am no longer required now that you are

returned to fulfill her need for . . . friends?"
guessed Blissford.

Lord Dorset positively beamed on him. "Exactly," he said.

Lord Blissford continued to smile, but his eyes narrowed. "You always were a conceited fellow," he observed. "Perhaps you should allow your wife to choose her friends herself."

"My wife may choose any friend she pleases," said Dorset stiffly. "But she has no need of a paramour."

Lord Blissford's smile had now turned superior, taunting, and Dorset's hand ached to put his fist in the middle of it. "I will thank you to stop trifling with my wife," he growled.

"But would she thank me?" countered Blissford lightly. "She may be yours in name, but I seriously doubt you possess her heart."

"What I do or do not possess is no affair of yours," snapped Dorset. "Leave Mary alone or I shall have to put a bullet through your chest."

He stalked off, leaving Lord Blissford with a light flush on his face and a considerably raised chin. "Conceited popinjay," muttered Blissford. "She is wasted on you."

Lord Dorset joined Sir Percy and his wife at the punch bowl. His head was beginning to ache, and the rather chill look he saw on his wife's face did nothing to ease it. She was, as usual, angry with him. And who could blame her? So far all he had done that evening was give a good imitation of a man bent an avoiding his wife. He had to do something to warm those cold, dark eyes. "Did I tell you yet how lovely you look this evening?" he tried.

"Guess I had best take myself off," said Sir Percy, setting down his punch cup.

Mary put a hand on his arm. "There is no need to leave, Percy."

"Oh, yes, there is," said Sir Percy. "I can see I ain't wanted."

"Nonsense," said Mary. "Jeremy is simply making conversation."

"Is that what you think?" demanded Dorset.

Sir Percy muttered a polite "Excuse me," and slipped away.

Mary watched him go, a nervous fluttering beginning in her chest.

"Mary." Her husband made her name sound like a caress. She turned her eyes to him. "You are the most beautiful creature I've ever seen," he said simply.

She blushed, suddenly feeling terribly self-conscious. "More beautiful than Lady Mumford?" she asked softly.

"It would be most cruel to Lady Mumford even to make a comparison," said the earl. "Mary, I am afraid I've gotten off to a very bad start as a husband," he said. "But I hope you won't hold that against me. I hope you'll give me the opportunity to earn your love." He picked up her hand and placed a kiss on it, the soft touch of his lips sending peculiar little prickles darting through her body.

She almost said, *You won that the first day I met you*. But he had tossed her aside as soon as they were wed. Now did he have her love? Ever since his return he'd done more to upset her than to make her happy. But if not love, then what emotion had so upset her when she'd watched him smile at Lady Mumford?

Lord Dorset rubbed his head.

"Jeremy, what is it?"

"I am afraid my head is beginning to hurt something fierce," he confessed.

"Then we must go home and put you to bed at once," said Mary. "I shall fetch Amanda."

They collected Amanda and Aubrey, and by the time they had donned their wraps and gotten into their carriage, Lord Dorset knew he was about to be very ill indeed. He remembered lying on a cot in a cottage in France, the thin blankets drenched with sweat, his teeth chattering, every inch of his body aching and burning. He remembered praying to die.

As his valet helped him out of his evening clothes, he shuddered violently and once more cursed the rotten luck that kept him from wooing his wife. He had been working so hard to slay his dragons. And now this. Here was one dragon he hadn't counted on. How long would this horrible thing lay him low? And what would happen between Mary and Blissford while he was down?

-Nine-

By THE NEXT morning the Earl of Dorset lay sweating and chilled under a mound of blankets. His head tossed back and forth on the pillow and he was muttering wildly in French. "Oh, dear," said Mary at the sight of him.

"Your ladyship might wish to send for the doctor," said his valet calmly.

A footman was duly dispatched and the Countess of Dorset took up vigil next to her husband's bed. Such devotion would have pleased the earl had he but been in his senses to know of it.

"'Tis the ague," pronounced the doctor. "We shall have to bleed him."

"No!" cried Mary.

"Mary!" cried the delirious earl.

The wrinkled little man stared at her as if she had taken leave of her senses. "Naturally your ladyship is upset by her husband's illness, but I

117

can assure you this is most necessary and will not harm him in the least."

"I am sorry," said Mary firmly, "but no." She could still see the doctor leeching her grandmother so freshly in her mind, even though she had only been a child at the time. The horrible little creatures sat on the old woman's arms, sucking out her life blood until, bloated with it, they fell off her. Once again the overwhelming feeling of loss surged over Mary. She felt as she had that day when she slipped into the bedroom to see the doctor pull the horrid, murderous things from her grandmother, then close the poor woman's eyes.

"But your ladyship," began the doctor.

"I shall take any powders you have to offer, but I will not allow you to leech my husband."

"I cannot be responsible for what happens if you do not allow me to do what I think best," cautioned the doctor.

"And I cannot allow you to use a method that I feel sure would be strongly detrimental to my husband's health," said Mary.

"Your ladyship. With all due respect, I have been a physician for twenty years, and I assure you this is a most common and beneficial practice."

Mary stood firm. She had not been raised in the country for nothing. She knew folk remedies, which she was sure the doctor would scorn, but that she had seen work miracles in the sickroom. She would trust her instincts.

She thanked the doctor for his time and sent him on his way, greatly insulted and full of dire predictions. Then she went to the kitchen and searched out the glass jar of dried herbs she had brought with her from Lincolnshire.

Half an hour later, with John to hold his master's head, she was spooning her herb tea down his lordship as best she could. Twice more that day she gave her lord her own private remedy, and in between doses laid cold, damp cloths on his forehead.

By evening he was no longer delirious, although still fevered and restless. Mary sat by his bed that night, spooning more tea into him, laying cloths on his head. Twice he weakly called her name. "I am here," she said, and patted his arm. "Rest."

Finally, in spite of her husband's tossing and fretful cries, she dozed in her chair. She stayed with him the next day, still ministering to him, her lips compressed into a grim line. Sometime that evening John insisted on relieving her. Reluctantly admitting her need for rest, she allowed herself to be sent from the sickroom after insisting John send for her if her husband should take a turn for the worse.

In the small hours of the morning she was again bending over her husband's bed, feeling his forehead, when a shadowy figure entered the sickroom and took her gently by the elbow. "Why such devotion to a man who does not appreciate you?" asked Lord Blissford. "Come away with me, Mary." He pulled her into his arms and kissed her. She could feel the warmth of his hard chest, feel his heart beating. "You love me. You know you do," he whispered, and kissed her again. And with this kiss she gave in. She threaded her hands through his golden locks and returned it with wild abandon. His lordship transferred his lips from her mouth to her neck, murmuring promises of undying passion.

From the sickbed came a low moan—Jeremy calling her name.

She put a hand to Lord Blissford's chest. "Jeremy," she said. "I must go to Jeremy."

She turned to go, but Lord Blissford caught her arm. "Why?" he asked. "Why go to someone who does not care for you?"

"Because I care for him," she cried. "Let me go! Let me—"

Mary's eyes flew open. She blinked and rubbed her eyes. "It was a dream," she told herself. "Only a dream."

Not wishing to dwell on either the dream or its implications, she rang for her abigail. She would dress and go see how Jeremy was doing this morning. Surely by now his fever must have broken. Perhaps he would be awake. With these thoughts and others like them she kept the image of Lord Blissford at bay until Randall arrived.

"Did you sleep well, my lady?" asked Randall in some concern.

"I did. Thank you," said Mary. Randall studied her mistress's face and Mary found herself blushing guiltily, as if Lord Blissford's name had been written on her forehead. "Please hurry," she said, ending all further discussion. "I wish to see how his lordship does this morning."

When she arrived at the sickroom, her husband was awake, his valet standing guard over him. He greeted her with an invalid's smile and she smiled back, her heart torn at the sight of his helplessness. "How do you feel?" she asked.

"Better," he said.

She felt his forehead. "Your fever has broken. Thank God."

"And thank you," said Dorset. "John tells me you sent the doctor packing and used your own remedies."

"I couldn't bear to see him bleed you," she said simply.

He smiled and closed his eyes. Within minutes he was asleep.

Mary gently pushed the dark curls from his forehead. How very like little boys men looked when they were sleeping, she thought, and felt a tender tug around her heart.

She left the invalid and made her way to the kitchen to see to it that a rich beef broth was brewed for her husband. Having seen to his needs, she made her way to the dining room for breakfast. There, she found both Aubrey and Amanda. "My, but I have slept late for both of you sleepyheads to beat me to breakfast," she said.

"How is the earl?" asked Amanda.

Mary was pleased by such an unselfish show of concern. "His fever has broken," she said.

"Do you think he will be well in time for Lady Wexford's card party?" Amanda wondered aloud, showing the real reason for her concern.

With an effort Mary put aside her irritation. Selfishness was an unfortunate affliction of youth. "I seriously doubt his lordship will be feeling up to any social outings by tomorrow night."

Amanda looked crestfallen.

"No need to fret," said Aubrey. "You have me to escort you."

"We still may go, mayn't we?" Amanda turned pleading eyes to Mary.

Mary hated to leave her husband when he had been so sick. It somehow seemed very frivolous and disloyal. And yet, how would she keep Amanda entertained if they did not go? She was sure Amanda was already feeling put upon because of her patroness's preoccupation with her husband. "I suppose we might still attend," said Mary hesitantly.

Amanda clapped her hands. "Oh, splendid! I shall wear my new blue gown with the blue rosettes and my beaded blue slippers."

"Best wear plenty of jewelry," cautioned Aubrey. "The way you play at cards you will, most like, have to wager it."

Amanda stuck out her tongue at him.

Mary ignored their banter, concentrating instead on her eggs, anxious to finish eating and get back to the sickroom.

She returned to her husband to find him still asleep, the ever-faithful John sitting next to him. "I shall take over," she whispered. "Why don't you try to get some rest."

The valet nodded and slipped from the room, leaving her ladyship to contemplate her sleeping husband and their life together. And what a strange life it had been thus far. She had been married a little over three years, yet she had not known love. And although there was something that tied her to Jeremy, she could not be sure whether it was simple gratitude for the gift of his name and title or something more. Was this love? And if so, what did she feel for Lord Blissford? Just remembering his recent improper advances was enough to cause a fluttering in her chest. How could she tell which man she really loved? How could she tell which man truly loved her? To which one should she give her heart's allegiance? Should she follow the advice given by Lady Melbourne to her daughter, Lady Cowper, and give loyalty to a lover, or should she cast her fate with her husband, the man who had so long neglected her? Lord Blissford had never neglected her. And her attraction for him could not be denied.

She studied her husband's sleeping face, struck again by how young he looked. And how much younger had he been when his father's death forced him to seek a wife? she suddenly wondered. Selfishness is an affliction of the young. Her earlier thought came back to defend her husband's callous treatment of his bride. He had been young and foolish. And selfish. Had he changed?

As if in answer to her question, he opened his eyes and smiled at her. "You're here," he murmured, and sighed.

Mary nodded and smiled encouragingly at him.

"I was just dreaming about you," he said.

"I hope it was pleasant," she replied, trying to keep her tone light.

"Mmm. Words cannot express." He sighed again. "And, alas, the body is too weak to show you."

Mary blushed. "You will be better soon," she said comfortingly. "Cook is making you some beef broth, which should help you regain your strength."

"I sincerely hope so." He sighed. "To think I have you here in my bedroom and I am too weak even to sit up, let alone hold you."

Mary was not sure what to say to this, but she was spared from answering as a footman came in bearing a tray with a steaming bowl of broth. "Ah. Here is your breakfast," said Mary.

His lordship eyed the bowl with disfavor. "'Tis not exactly a steak, is it?"

"No," she agreed. "But I am afraid trying to chew a steak would only weaken you further. Besides, the nourishment is in the broth." She took the bowl. "Now, drink up," she commanded, and put a spoon to his mouth.

The following day his lordship was sitting up in bed and had progressed from broth to tea and toast. "If I promise to behave myself, might I have something that at least resembles meat tomorrow?" he asked.

His wife smiled. "I am sure by tomorrow you will wish to join us for dinner."

"I wish I felt up to joining you tonight." Dorset sighed, leaning back among his pillows. "I am afraid this illness has left me weak as a kitten."

"I wish you were feeling better, too," said Mary. "I am afraid I am not much looking forward to attending Lady Wexford's card party without you."

The mention of Lady Wexford's party took the smile from Dorset's face. "Did you send for Percy?" he asked.

Mary nodded. "But I wish you had not asked me to do so. It seems rather unfair to expect Percy to upset what plans he might have had for tonight simply to accompany Aubrey and Amanda and myself to a card party."

The earl nodded. "I am well aware of your feelings on this subject," he said. "But I will feel so much better if I know Percy is there looking out for your interests. Many a sharper has slipped into a card party before and fleeced his share of fools. Even among our own ranks there are those to whom winning is everything, and who would not be above a little dishonest play. And while I do not worry so much about your skills, I frankly think Aubrey and Amanda will need watching."

Mary sighed. "I suppose you are right," she said. "I hope it may not prove a great inconvenience for Percy. It seems we have embroiled him much in our affairs this season."

That evening Sir Percy paid a quick visit to the sickroom, reassuring the earl that accompanying Lady Dorset and her charges to Lady Wexford's party would not be in the least inconvenient. In fact, he had been planning to attend. "Be glad to keep an eye on Miss Tuttle," he informed his cousin.

"And on Mary," said Dorset. "Especially on Mary. I am sure that rake Blissford will be there, looking for an opportunity to dally with her." Sir Percy rubbed his head and his cousin studied him. "Are you quite all right, old fellow?" he asked.

"You ask me to watch the cub, who'll drop the blunt like he's Midas himself, and Miss Tuttle, who don't know what's trump, and keep Blissford away from Mary, and then you ask me if I am all right?" He shook his head. "Got an ache in the old brain box just from thinking about it."

Sir Percy left the earl fretting in his bed as he remembered the headache that had announced his own illness. He hoped his cousin's pain in the brain box was simply from thinking of the challenge that lay before him and not the portent of an illness that would render him useless to Mary long before the evening was over.

-*Ten*-

LADY WEXFORD WAS no Crockford, but her card parties offered the ladies as deep play as they'd ever be allowed and the gentlemen high enough stakes to make the evening tolerably interesting. And the presence of women such as the Duchess of Goldborough, who was so addicted to play she would gamble away her favors when her money ran out, also kept things lively. Lady Wexford enjoyed lively parties. In fact, Lady Wexford enjoyed making mischief, and this particular evening she had invited such a mixture of guests as was bound to ensure it.

Aubrey and Amanda entered her ladyship's drawing room ready for excitement. Amanda, on catching sight of the tables and chairs placed about the room, took Aubrey's arm and gave it a squeeze. "Whist and loo, and her ladyship said she would have a table for rouge et noir. I have never played it, but I hear it is all the crack. Oh, there it is! This will be such fun,'' she predicted.

Mary followed them in with a feeling of foreboding perched on her shoulder. She was not sure that the evening would be fun at all. She looked at the collection of fine-looking ladies and gentlemen milling about, all of them addicted to gambling. She knew many of the women had left their husbands dallying at the opera house and come here to meet their lovers. What a fast set she had fallen in with since opening up a gambling establishment! This was hardly the proper place for a young lady making her come-out, especially when that young lady was Amanda.

Aubrey and Amanda together at a gambling party spelled trouble, Mary was sure. Percy would be of little help, for she was sure he was feeling unwell. He had been subdued in the carriage on the way over, and now, although he was smiling, she could tell it was an effort. She wished Jeremy had felt up to coming. He would have known how to keep Aubrey and Amanda in line. She was not at all sure she could. Oh, why ever had she accepted Lady Wexford's invitation in the first place! If only she had been brave enough to use her husband's illness as an excuse not to come. She knew they were only here because she had been too cowardly to face Amanda's pouts and pleas. Well, now she would pay for her cowardice.

She braced herself for the ordeal that lay ahead and smiled at her hostess. "My dear, you look positively stunning tonight," gushed Lady Wexford.

Mary took in her hostess's clinging gown. Damped. "I shall be no match for you," she said politely.

Lady Wexford smoothed the material over her generous curves with satisfaction. "One tries one's hardest to compete with the beautiful Lady Dorset," she said. Her smile turned mischievous. "There is someone here most anxious to spend the evening in your company."

Mary saw Lord Blissford approaching and her heart gave a sick flop. Oh, dear, she thought. Here, indeed, was trouble.

Lady Wexford disappeared as he bowed over her hand. "Now my evening is complete," he said. "We are partnered for whist. I feel lucky. Are you feeling skillful?"

Mary said she hoped so. She certainly wasn't feeling lucky. She looked around the room. People were beginning to sit down. She watched

Amanda head for the rouge et noir table, Aubrey close behind her. Oh, dear. Why could they not just be content with whist? Sir Percy was taking a seat at the table next to hers. At least she could keep an eye on him from where she sat. If he showed signs of feeling worse she would take them all home. It would make a wonderful excuse to leave. And she almost hoped he felt very ill very soon.

Liveried footmen walked among the tables, delivering decks of cards and supplying the guests with punch. The murmur of polite conversation floated about the room. The evening's play had begun.

Lord Blissford smiled at Mary. He threw out his first card and winked at her.

She smiled back weakly and wished she were already home. As soon as they stopped for supper, she would convince Percy that he was too unwell to stay any longer and they would leave. She only hoped Amanda would not gamble away what was left of her pin money. There were still four weeks left in the season, and it would be a long four weeks for them all if Amanda had no money left to spend.

The evening wore on, and as more wine and iced champagne were consumed the quiet conversation got louder and the laughter more raucous. Mary caught sight of a gentleman tucking a wad of money into a lady's bodice. The woman blew him a kiss. Another man had pulled a lady onto his lap and was nibbling his way down her neck while he waited to play his card. Mary's eyes widened. She looked to see if Amanda had seen this shocking behavior. Amanda was on the other side of the room, too caught up in the game to notice anything. Mary turned her attention back to the game at hand, trying to ignore her surroundings. She felt a foot creeping up her leg and jumped. Lord Blissford pursed his mouth, sending her a silent kiss, and she swallowed hard. Would this evening never end?

A footman came to their table. "Lady Dorset would like a cup of champagne punch," said Blissford. He smiled at her. "You are looking very warm, my dear."

"Yes," agreed the woman sitting next to her. "And how you can sit with your shawl wrapped around you I cannot imagine. I am finding it uncomfortably close in here."

Lord Blissford rose and came behind her. "Allow me," he said, and slid the shawl from her shoulders. The man on her right leered appreciatively as the shawl fell away from her low-cut gown. Mary felt as if she were being stripped naked and flushed a fiery red. The footman returned with her punch and she drank it gratefully, for she was now feeling very warm indeed. "Perhaps another cup," suggested Lord Blissford, and Mary promised herself if she escaped this evening's madness, she would refuse all future invitations from Lady Wexford.

Across the room Amanda was desperately trying to hit a winning streak. She had lost all her pin money and her bracelet long ago. Her earrings, too, were gone. Aubrey, sure her luck was bound to turn any moment, had given her more money. But now he, too, was out of funds. She watched as the dealer started laying out the cards, sure the rouge row was going to be nearer the magic number of thirty-one cards than the noir row. She knew this time she could win back all she'd lost. "Stop!" she cried, jumping up and grabbing the dealer's hand. "Five hundred pounds on rouge."

"But Miss Tuttle, you do not have five hundred pounds," the dealer reminded her.

"I will vouch for her," said Aubrey.

"You have five hundred pounds?" The man was plainly skeptical.

"I shall give you my vowel," said Aubrey stiffly.

The dealer looked to Lady Wexford, who had drifted over. She smiled at Aubrey and nodded to the man.

"Five hundred pounds on rouge," he said, and resumed laying out the cards.

Amanda counted with him, hovering over the table and holding her breath.

"Noir wins," he said at last.

Amanda fell back into her chair in shock. "Oh, dear," she breathed.

Sir Percy was having trouble focusing on his cards, the diamonds and hearts blurring into similar-looking red spots. He looked up. The red spots were not only on his cards. They danced in the air about his head. His forehead felt damp. Hot in here, he realized. So hot. He turned to where Mary sat. The red spots danced on her face as she looked at him in concern. "Percy," she said. "Are you feeling all right?"

Her voice seemed to come from far away. "Not feeling quite the thing," he confessed.

Mary was not feeling quite the thing herself. Her head was fuzzy. Someone's toes were exploring her thigh. It tickled. She giggled, then stopped, shocked. Was that really she who had just giggled? She looked again at Percy, who was trying to stand. He swayed. "Percy!" she cried. "Oh, dear. We must get him home. I am afraid he has taken ill." She stood, and found she was swaying dizzily herself. She grabbed the chair for support. Lord Blissford jumped from his seat and caught her arms, steadying her. "Percy, we must get you home," she informed her cousin.

"Allow me to help you collect your party," said Lord Blissford. He bent and retrieved her shawl, which had fallen to the floor. He draped it over her shoulders and she thought she felt the touch of his lips on her neck. "I really must go," she said, and pulled away.

"I shall find your brother and Miss Tuttle," offered Blissford. "I am sorry our evening has come to such a premature end," he whispered.

Mary didn't know what to say to this. Fortunately she was spared having to say anything at all, as his lordship left her. She took Sir Percy's arm and together they weaved their way to the door.

Amanda and Aubrey had left the rouge et noir table and now they stood a little apart from the company, each wearing a worried expression. "What are we to do?" whimpered Amanda. "Neither of us has five hundred pounds."

Aubrey shrugged. "I have some property in Lincolnshire," he said. "Maybe her ladyship would accept that."

"Heavens! That is surely worth more than five hundred pounds," said Amanda. "You shouldn't give away your property."

Aubrey thought. "Then I shall have to pawn something."

"But what have you to pawn worth five hundred pounds?" asked Amanda.

Aubrey looked down at his cravat. "This stickpin," he suggested.

Amanda eyed it dubiously. "I am not sure that is worth five hundred pounds."

Aubrey considered. "I shall find something," he said.

"But what?"

"If I have to, I can pawn something of Mary's—get it back out when I'm a little more plump in the pocket."

Amanda bit her lip.

"She won't mind," said Aubrey. "But don't tell her. No sense worrying her, especially when I'll be getting it back within a week or so."

A voice from behind them made the guilty couple jump. "I am afraid Sir Percival is not feeling well. Her ladyship has asked me to fetch you to her," said Lord Blissford.

"Very well," said Aubrey. "Come, Amanda."

"Do you think he heard us talking?" whispered Amanda as they preceded Lord Blissford out of the room.

Aubrey sincerely hoped not. He shook his head and tried to look unconcerned.

Lord Blissford said nothing to confirm or deny Miss Tuttle's suspicions, but Lady Wexford noticed he was wearing a smile that could only be described as naughty. She bade her last guests adieu and looked at Blissford coyly. "And did you enjoy yourself this evening, my lord?"

"I always enjoy myself at your parties, my lady," he said, planting a kiss on her palm.

"I fear I am no longer your lady," she said, sighing. "I haven't been since Lady Dorset came to town. Did you see? Her little protégée dipped rather deep tonight."

"And the young man gallantly offered to pay her debt?" finished his lordship.

Lady Wexford nodded. "If he weren't related to Dorset, I'd never have allowed it. But I know Dorset will stand bluff."

Lord Blissford nodded and his smile widened. "Most likely he will. One way or another."

Once in the carriage all four occupants leaned back against the squabs with a sigh of relief.

"Percy, I think you had best come home with us," said Mary. "If you have caught that terrible sickness Jeremy had, it will never do for you to stay alone in your town house with only the servants to attend you."

Sir Percy was, by now, feeling too weak to argue. "Most kind," he muttered, and leaned his splitting head against the side of the coach.

Mary's head was hurting, too. So was her conscience. She was going to be in terrible trouble if she was not careful. She tried not to think of the sensations Lord Blissford had created in her with his surreptitious movements under the card table earlier. Shame on him! And shame on her, too. She must be encouraging him somehow. She knew she had flirted with him when first she'd met him. He was so handsome, so attentive. And she had been so lonely. But now her husband was home, prepared to make things up to her, and things had changed. Hadn't they? And Jeremy was every bit as handsome as Lord Blissford. And every bit as kind and attentive. So why did Lord Blissford affect her so strongly?

She could find no sensible answer to her question, and as the carriage stopped and the footman was letting down the steps, she gave up thinking about it, sternly shooing thoughts of Lord Blissford away and setting her mind to the task of seeing everyone to their respective beds. Percy, she knew, would need nursing.

While the servants were settling him she went to check on her husband. She peered into the bedroom and found him sleeping soundly and didn't know whether to be relieved or disappointed that he was not awake to talk with her.

Mary gathered cool water and cloths and a sleeping draft and found Percy lying with chattering teeth under a pile of blankets. "S-so cold," he stuttered. "And my whole body aches."

"I know," she said gently. "We shall have you well in no time. Drink this. It will help you sleep."

It was a long night for Mary. She stayed with Percy until the small hours of the morning, then sought her own bed, too tired to worry about Lord Blissford.

She was still sleeping when her stepbrother slipped into the library. He moved to the far side of the room and stood before a portrait on the wall. He studied it for several moments, running his fingers along its ornately carved frame. At last he found what he was looking for. The picture swung out from the wall to reveal a small cupboard. Aubrey smiled and reached in. "Family secrets," he muttered happily, and pulled out a thin, rectangular box. He opened it, and there in its satin lining lay an ornate necklace of emeralds and pearls. He pocketed it and shut the secret door, then slipped from the library and out of the house, the bulge in his jacket pocket barely discernible.

-Eleven-

AUBREY TURNED QUICKLY into Cranbourn Alley, anxious to be done with his business. His conscience smote him, for he knew he shouldn't be pawning the Dorset necklace. And he knew if the earl ever found out he'd taken the thing to old Jew King, there'd be the devil to pay. But Amanda needed his help. And besides, he knew he could win the money back within the week. As soon as he had the blunt, he'd return the necklace and no one need ever be the wiser.

As the jeweler's establishment came in sight, Aubrey received a shock. There, lounging outside the door, was none other than the Earl of Blissford. "Oh, Lord," muttered Aubrey under his breath. Too late to duck back down the street. The curst fellow had seen him. Well, Blissford need not know what he was about.

Aubrey sauntered up the street toward the

door, trying his best to look like a man of the world. "Hullo, Lord Blissford," he said, and tipped his hat.

"Well, Mr. Mayhill," said his lordship. "What a coincidence. Here am I, just waiting to meet a friend, and who should I encounter but Miss Tuttle's brave rescuer of last night."

Aubrey found himself blushing. The fact that Blissford was older and a head taller did nothing to eradicate Aubrey's feeling like a schoolboy caught in a prank.

"The veriest nothing," said Aubrey. "If you'll excuse me." He tried to brush by.

Blissford blocked his path. "Perhaps pawning the family jewels might not be such a good idea," he suggested.

"I am merely here on business," said Aubrey haughtily.

"A rather risky business," suggested Blissford.

"I am sure what I am doing can be no concern of yours, sir," said Aubrey stiffly.

"Oh, but it is," corrected his lordship. "As your sister is a particular friend of mine, I feel it concerns me very much. I should hate to see her caused any grief by a well-meant but rash action. You see, if you pawn the Dorset emeralds—it is the Dorset necklace you have, is it not?" Aubrey's blush confirmed Blissford's suspicions. "Well," continued his lordship, "I am afraid your brother-in-law will hold your sister very much to blame."

Aubrey bit his lip. "What am I to do?" he cried at last.

"Allow me to assist you," said his lordship. He produced a wad of bills. "Consider this a loan between gentlemen. You may repay me when it is convenient. No interest." He nodded toward the shop behind them. "Which is a much better deal than old Jew King would give you."

This was too good to be true. How fortunate to have encountered a friend with Mary's best interests at heart! "Very well, sir. And thank you." Aubrey took the money.

Lord Blissford held out his hand. "I shall be happy to see the necklace gets safely back to your sister."

Aubrey was suddenly hesitant to give the necklace up. After all, if he gave the thing to Blissford, Mary was bound to find out how it had come to disappear in the first place. "I can return it and none the wiser," he said.

His lordship looked unconvinced. "Are you sure of that? Why take a chance on being found returning it. Best let me discreetly give it to your sister."

Aubrey considered this. The thought of being caught by his brother-in-law with his hand in the safe was not a pleasant one. Discretion was what was called for here. Aubrey was sure his lordship would be discreet. And he would explain how Aubrey had only been trying to help Amanda. He gave the necklace to Lord Blissford. "Thank you," he said. "It is very kind of you to help us."

"Pray, don't mention it," said his lordship with a smile.

Mary had checked on Sir Percy and found him fevered and restless. She promised to look in on him after breakfast and left him to go check on her husband.

She peeked in to find him sitting up in bed reading a book. Other than looking a little gaunt, he appeared well. He smiled at the sight of her. "Good morning," he said.

She entered the room, feeling suddenly shy. "How are you feeling?"

"As if I am going to live. I think, perhaps, I shall leave the sickroom today." He gave her a quizzical look. "If the doctor permits."

Mary smiled. "I am sure it wouldn't hurt you to be up for a little while," she said.

He patted the bed. "Will you sit awhile and tell me how your evening was?"

Mary's mind raced frantically as she tried to think what she could possibly dredge up from that disastrous evening to tell her husband. "The

146

evening ended rather early," she said. "I am afraid your cousin became very ill. He is here now."

Dorset sighed. "I feared yesterday he might be coming down with something. Does he have what I had?"

Mary nodded. "It seems so. His illness is not as violent as yours was, however. I imagine he will be up and about in another day."

"That is good." Lord Dorset studied his wife. "Did you enjoy your evening before poor Percy took ill?"

Mary shrugged noncommittally. "I enjoy cards," she said. What else to tell him? She was not about to confide the warring feelings Lord Blissford's amorous behavior had stirred up in her. She was equally loath to relate her concern that Amanda and Aubrey may have gambled away more than they should have. She hated to confess that she had made an error in judgment in allowing herself to become part of Lady Wexford's fast set, but she knew she would not wish her husband to hear of some of the goings-on at her ladyship's party and think his wife was a willing party to it. "I am afraid," she said, "that on becoming better acquainted with Lady Wexford and her friends, I find myself not so very fond of their company."

"And why is that?" prompted Dorset.

"They are rather a fast set. I don't think their influence at all good on Amanda." Or on myself, she thought.

"Was Lord Blissford there?" asked her husband casually.

Mary hoped the warmth she was suddenly feeling on her cheeks was not a betraying blush. "Yes," she said. "He sat at my table for whist." Her husband frowned. "But his lordship and I did not have much chance to visit," she added quickly, "for we left long before supper was served."

"Pity," said his lordship. He grinned at her. "I am a jealous fellow," he confessed.

"I am flattered," said his wife.

Dorset sighed and leaned his head back against the pillows.

"I have tired you," said Mary, instantly contrite.

"I could never tire of you," he said.

She smiled and felt her cheeks growing warmer still. "I shall have some breakfast sent up to you. Then perhaps you can rest awhile."

Mary went downstairs to breakfast with a light step. When her husband had first returned, she hadn't dared risk giving him her heart again. He had broken it so thoroughly after chivalrously marrying her and then unchivalrously fleeing. Her head had cautioned her to beware. But hearts give themselves where they will, despite the warnings of the head. Indeed, if she were to be honest, she knew she'd have to admit that he had always held her heart strings, in spite of all she had tried to tell herself to the contrary. Now she was sure it was her husband she loved. And she felt equally convinced that he had come to love her as well, and not just for her beauty. Surely his illness had forged something between them that was stronger than mere attraction and deeper than anything she could ever have with Lord Blissford. Mary smiled, feeling as if the sunshine that had shone through her husband's bedroom window had followed her down the stairs.

The sight of Amanda sitting alone in the dining room wearing a troubled look on her face took some of the shine off Mary's morning. Oh, dear, she thought. How much had the child lost the previous night? "Is something troubling you?" Mary asked.

"Oh, no," said Amanda quickly. "I am a little tired. That is all."

"Aubrey has not yet come down to breakfast?" asked Mary.

Amanda squirmed in her seat. "I have not seen him," she said.

At that moment Aubrey himself put in an

appearance. "Well," he said heartily, "I see everyone is finally up. I've been up for hours."

Amanda looked at him questioningly and he nodded slightly. Her face relaxed and she became quite cheerful.

Very peculiar, thought Mary. What have they been up to?

She had no time to find out, however. They were still at breakfast when they had a morning caller—Lord Norton, wishing to speak with Lord Dorset. "I am very sorry," said Mary. "My husband has been unwell. If you would care to call back in two days' time, I am sure he will be well enough then to receive you."

His lordship bowed, bestowed an enormous box of comfits on Amanda, and left.

"Oh dear," wailed Amanda, throwing the box down unopened. "He wishes to marry me."

"Here now," protested Aubrey. "You can't marry Amanda to that old bird. She would be miserable."

"This is hardly the Middle Ages," said Mary. "I am sure if Amanda doesn't wish to marry Lord Norton, she needn't do so."

Neither Aubrey nor Amanda looked convinced of this, both obviously preferring the roles of star-crossed lovers. "If I were betrothed to such a man, I should drink poison," vowed Amanda.

"Good Lord!" cried Aubrey. "What would you want to do a hen-witted thing like that for? The sensible thing would be for someone to challenge the fellow to a duel and run him through with a sword."

"Whom are you planning to impale?" inquired Lord Dorset, strolling into the room.

"Jeremy! What are you doing up?" scolded Mary.

"Merely enjoying a change of scene," said his lordship. "I think I am so weak because I have had nothing these past three days but broth and toast. And I decided I should prefer to take breakfast in the company of someone other than myself."

"Are you planning to marry Amanda to Norton?" demanded Aubrey.

Lord Dorset considered his plate. "I am planning on helping Amanda achieve a suitable match," he said. "I should think Lord Norton would make an admirable husband."

"He has clammy hands," said Amanda miserably.

"That, indeed, is a problem," agreed Dorset, and changed the subject. Turning to his wife, he suggested they attend the opera the following night. "I have a strong desire to see you dressed as I saw you that first night I returned, with your hair done up and the Dorset necklace glittering on your lovely neck.''

At these words Aubrey's eyes bulged. Jeremy did not see his brother-in-law's face, but Mary did. Her smile shrank, and with a puzzled look his lordship followed her gaze to her brother, who was already rising, pronouncing himself as stuffed as a Christmas goose. Miss Tuttle, too, was feeling a sudden need to leave the table. "I think I shall see if my maid would care for these comfits," she said, making good her escape.

"You do not care for the idea of attending the opera?" asked his lordship.

Mary recovered. "I should love to attend the opera with you. Let us see how you are feeling tomorrow," she said.

Something was afoot. Dorset knew it. And it involved the cub. Blast! Well, before the week was out, he would have both Aubrey and Miss Tuttle's futures firmly sealed and both of them out of his hair. Consoling himself with that thought, he buttered a muffin, determined to gain enough strength by the following night to woo his wife properly.

The simple act of eating breakfast exhausted him and forced him back to his bed.

He left his wife at the table alone, calmly pouring herself another cup of tea. But once he was gone, the facade of tranquillity fell away.

Lady Luck

Biting her lip, she rose and quietly made her way to the library, hoping with each step that she was wrong. She ran to the secret cupboard and looked inside. Frantically she felt among the various papers and boxes, but to no avail. What she sought was gone.

-Twelve-

TRYING TO REMAIN calm, Mary tugged at the bell-pull. The butler appeared and was dispatched to find Aubrey and bring him to the mistress without delay. Mary took a seat to wait and found she couldn't remain in it. She began to pace.

She was still pacing when her brother entered the room, which he correctly interpreted as a sign of trouble ahead. "I was just about to go out," he said. "Perhaps we can talk later?"

"Of a certainty we shall talk now," said Mary firmly. "Where is it?"

"Where is what?"

"You know very well what I mean," snapped Mary. "Oh, Aubrey," she cried. "What have you done with the necklace? Tell me you have not pawned it."

"Well, no. Not really. Blissford has it."

"Lord Blissford?" asked Mary faintly.

"I was going to pawn it," confessed Aubrey. His sister collapsed into the nearest chair. "But 'tis all right, Mary. I didn't need to. Blissford happened along and gave me the money to pay Amanda's debt. He's going to return the necklace to you, so everything will be all right and tight and no harm done."

"No harm done?" echoed his sister. "Aubrey, have you any idea what you have done?" she moaned.

"I was only trying to help Amanda," he said stiffly. "And besides, I'm sure Blissford will call sometime today and return the necklace to you. You'll have it in plenty of time to wear to the opera tomorrow."

"And what if I do not?" demanded his sister. Aubrey had nothing to say to this. "Oh, go away," she said angrily. "I am quite out of patience with you."

Aubrey left in a huff and Mary got up and resumed her pacing. Why would Lord Blissford loan her irresponsible brother such a large sum of money? And if he merely wished to help, why take the necklace? Why not allow Aubrey to return it? She remembered his lordship's behavior toward her the last time they met, and shivered. Did an ulterior motive lurk behind his generous gesture?

Mary wasn't the only one in the household with a troubled spirit. In the hall Aubrey met a teary-eyed Amanda. One look at her face made him forget his own troubles. "Amanda, what is the matter?"

"I am sure his lordship means to marry me to Lord Norton. What shall I do?" She looked up at him forlornly.

Here was one person who didn't think of him as a child. Amanda knew he was a capable man of the world. She depended on him. He couldn't let her down. "Nothing for it but to elope," he said. Removing himself from his brother-in-law's angry reach for a time sounded nearly as good as helping Amanda. Besides, he was fond of the chit and he'd always had a desire to see Scotland.

"Elope?" Amanda was saying. "With whom?"

"With me, of course," said Aubrey. "None of these other men care for you like I do."

"Oh, yes," breathed Amanda, all smiles. "How romantic!"

"Good," said Aubrey, all business. "We shall leave tomorrow night." He turned to leave.

"But when tomorrow night?" she asked. "And how shall we elope?"

"I don't know yet," admitted Aubrey. "But leave all to me."

That afternoon Aubrey visited Sir Percy's sickroom. "How are you feeling?" he ventured.

Percy was on fire and his head hurt like the devil. "Foul," he said. Aubrey nodded and bit his lip. Percy did not feel like company, particularly the company of a rival. "Something particular you wanted?" he asked.

"Oh, well, now you mention it, I had hoped you might loan me your carriage and a little blunt. I have an important errand I need to run for Miss Tuttle. She is in need of some assistance."

Percy closed his eyes, trying to remember the events of Lady Wexford's party. Had Miss Tuttle dipped too deep? Was she trying to keep it a secret from Mary? Why the devil had he gone and fallen ill? Here he was supposed to have been keeping an eye on everyone for Jeremy and he hadn't the foggiest notion what had happened that evening. He supposed he should question Aubrey about what he needed the money for, ask him to confess what had happened at the party and what part he was playing in the thing. But it was all too much for his fevered brain. He just wanted to sleep.

"By all means," he mumbled. Maybe Miss Tuttle would be grateful to him for loaning the money to help her out of her difficulties. Perhaps when she heard of his good deed, she would see him in a new light. Percy's eyelids fell and he heard Aubrey's voice as if from a great distance, thanking him, telling him what a good fellow he was.

Sir Percy slept the rest of the day. Late in the afternoon his cousin came to visit him. "How do you feel, old fellow?" asked Dorset, perching on a corner of the bed.

Percy sighed. "Better," he said. "I'm sorry I didn't keep a better watch on Mary for you."

His lordship shrugged. "She seems to have survived. But I suspect something is up. The Dorset necklace is missing."

"What!" croaked Percy.

Dorset nodded. "I have just checked. I suspect my brother-in-law has pawned it. Do you remember anything about the Wexfords' party that might help me piece together this puzzle?"

Sir Percy rubbed his head. That evening had been cursed. "Don't know," he muttered. "But I do know Miss Tuttle is in some kind of trouble. The cub wants to help her."

"Heaven help us all," said his lordship.

"I think she dipped deep," said Percy.

"I cannot imagine her doing otherwise," said Dorset. "And I suspect there is a connection between Miss Tuttle's gambling debts and the disappearance of my family's heirloom neck-lace."

Percy looked at him with a troubled expression. "Afraid I let you down all around," he said.

"Nonsense," said Dorset.

"What will you do?" asked Percy.

"I have already sent a man to make discreet inquiries. It may be a simple matter of redeeming it from a jeweler."

"Unless a private party has intervened," mused Sir Percy. His brows knit.

"What is it?" asked his lordship.

"Either way it don't make sense. If Aubrey pawned the necklace, what did he want my blunt for?" A look of determination settled on Percy's face and he threw back the blankets and made an effort to get up.

"Here now!" protested the earl. "What the devil do you think you are doing?"

"Got to find Aubrey. Find out what's up," muttered Sir Percy. His head began to spin and he clapped his hands to it.

"All you are going to find is some more rest," said Dorset, shoving him firmly back against the pillows. "Look at you. You've still got a fever and you are dizzy to boot."

"You need help," insisted Percy.

"You will be more help to me if you concentrate on getting well," said his lordship.

Percy sighed heavily and shut his eyes. "Something havey-cavey is going on."

His lordship had to agree. Well, he would get to the bottom of this. Perhaps he should start by accompanying his wife to the rout she planned to attend. "John," he said to his valet that evening, "be so good as to lay out something for me to wear to a rout."

John was not one to worry and fret about his master's health. He did as he was bade.

His lordship's wife, however, was not quite so unflappable as his valet. She was quick to object when his lordship showed up at the dinner table dressed for an evening out and announced his intention of accompanying her and Amanda to the rout.

Fear more than concern prompted her to object to her husband's plans. All day she had waited for Lord Blissford to call on her and return the necklace, but she had waited in vain. She had hoped to speak with him at the rout. But how would she ever be able to get back the necklace from Lord Blissford with her husband hovering over her? "It is only the first day you have been out of bed," she protested. "Surely it will do you no good to be out in the night air so soon."

"I think it will do me a great deal of good," said the earl. "I have been cooped up in the

161

house far too long. And besides, I don't see Aubrey. Obviously he does not mean to accompany you. I shall take his place."

"You will tire yourself and then not have the strength to go out tomorrow night," she said.

His lordship was already tired, but he had no intention of confessing that to his wife. For some reason she wished him not to come. Could the reason be a certain emerald necklace? "I shall certainly do nothing to endanger our evening together at the opera," he promised.

"It will be a most boring affair," Mary predicted.

"I shall not be bored in your company," he countered.

Mary gave up. She tried to remain calm, concentrating instead on her soup. She would think of some way to speak with Lord Blissford that night. She had to.

After dinner the ladies went upstairs to make last-minute adjustments on their toilettes and to don their capes and gloves. Mary shooed off Amanda's abigail and shut the door. "I must have a word with you," she said.

Amanda turned pale. "Yes?" she said cautiously.

"I am afraid my brother has been rather rash,"

Mary began. Amanda sank into the nearest chair and Mary hurried on, anxious not to upset the child. "He has given something valuable, something that should not have left our family, over to a friend. I am going to have to speak with that person sometime tonight and I am afraid I must ask your assistance in this matter."

A look of relief swept over Amanda's face. "Of course. What can I do to help?"

"You must keep his lordship occupied while I speak with this person."

"But how will I know when to keep him occupied? And who is this other person?"

"It is Lord Blissford," said Mary, trying not to look like a woman with a guilty secret. "When he enters the room, you must find some way to distract my husband so I can speak with his lordship."

"But how?" asked Amanda.

Mary shook her head impatiently. "I don't know," she said. "You will have to think of something."

The rout was a crush. It seemed to Lord Dorset that they stood for hours simply waiting to greet their hostess. The rooms were crowded and food was already scarce. Miss Tuttle looked bored. Good, he thought. Perhaps they could make an early night of it.

163

Miss Tuttle caught sight of someone across the room and shot a look at Mary. "Is it warm in here?" she asked suddenly. "I feel very warm." She unfurled her fan and began to ply it.

"Perhaps some punch," suggested Mary. "I see a footman. I shall fetch you some."

Before the earl could stop her, his wife had flung herself into the crowd. He followed her progress and noted she passed a footman bearing a tray of punch cups. She was heading for a tall man with golden hair. "Blissford," growled the earl, and made to follow her.

A small, plump hand grabbed his arm. "I feel faint," announced Miss Tuttle. "Could we sit down?"

"Here is a chair. Why don't you rest and I shall see about fetching you some punch."

"But your wife has already gone to get me some," objected Amanda. "Pray, don't leave me. I am very much afraid I shall swoon."

His lordship sat, the picture of reluctant chivalry. The sight of someone in the crowd brought a smile to his face. "Mother!" he cried. "How delightful to see you." He freed himself from Amanda's grip and jumped up. "Miss Tuttle is not feeling quite the thing. Perhaps you would care to bear her company for a few moments while I fetch her some punch."

"But Mary has gone to fetch me punch," protested Amanda.

"She appears to have forgotten her mission," said his lordship. "I shall return." Miss Tuttle grabbed his coattail. "You must not leave me," she commanded. "I am about to faint."

"Mother will support you," promised the earl.

He pulled his coat free and made good his escape. "Oh, dear." Amanda sighed. "I hope I kept him long enough."

Her ladyship raised a questioning eyebrow. "And why, pray, were you to keep him?" she asked.

Amanda turned a deep crimson. "Oh, no reason," she said. "I am feeling ever so much better, but I am still thirsty. I think I shall get some punch. May I bring you some?"

"By all means," said her ladyship agreeably. She sat back and scanned the crowd. At the edge of the mass of bodies she caught a glimpse of her daughter-in-law slipping out the French doors on the far side of the room in the company of Lord Blissford. "How very curious," she murmured.

Mary wasted no time once she and his lordship were alone. "I believe you have something that belongs to me. I should be grateful if you would return it and allow me to pay my brother's debt to you."

"I should be happy to bring it to you," said his lordship, taking her hand. She watched, mesmerized as he kissed it. "Perhaps now that he is recovered from his illness, your husband plans to attend his club one night this week."

Mary yanked away her hand. "My husband plans to attend the opera with me tomorrow night," she said coldly. "And he wishes me to wear the Dorset necklace."

Lord Blissford considered this. "You do face a dilemma."

"You must give it to me immediately," insisted Mary.

"My dear, I have every intention of returning your necklace to you. You are most fortunate I stumbled upon your brother in front of Jew King's shop. Else you might never have regained it."

Heavens! If Aubrey had actually pawned the necklace, who knows if she'd have been able to find it. "And I am most grateful for your kindness," said Mary sincerely.

"Are you?" asked his lordship softly. He put an arm around her and pulled her close. "Are you truly grateful?" His lips touched her cheek. "I should like you to show me how very grateful you are."

She stiffened. "What is your meaning, sir?"

"I think you can guess."

The beast! she thought. "I do not wish to have the necklace that badly," she informed him.

"Oh? Would you really wish to have to explain to your husband what happened to his family's treasure? And do you really think he cares so much that he would forgive you its loss?"

Mary looked at him with disdain. "You, sir, are a villain."

Blissford shook his head. "No. I am merely a man who has long desired a woman and now"—he shrugged fatalistically—"has found a way to win her. If I must buy your affection, so be it. For once you have spent a night with me, I fancy you will no longer care for the regard of one who has so long neglected you."

"If you wish to win my undying love, why not give me the necklace now?" pleaded Mary.

"Why? Because I do not have it with me." He smiled wickedly at her and kissed her ear, sending a pleasant tingle through her body and a guilty flush to her face. "I shall bring it to you," he whispered. Mary said nothing and he continued, "Only think what a scandal it would be if word got out that you had carelessly allowed your brother to pawn the family necklace. And it would get out, you know. These things have a way of surfacing. Come, Mary. I seek only to help you. Why are you fighting me so?"

Mary bit her lip and bowed her head, resigned to her fate. "Very well," she whispered. "Bring the necklace to me."

"Perhaps tomorrow night?" he suggested.

"We were to go to the opera," said Mary.

"Perhaps you had best send your husband on to the opera alone. When he returns, you can be wearing the necklace."

Mary looked at Lord Blissford and wondered how she could ever have had any regard for such a scoundrel.

He was regarding her quizzically. "Such a show of virtue," he teased. "One would think you do not care for me in the least," he said.

"I don't!" Mary insisted.

"Methinks the lady doth protest too much," he replied. He smiled. "I know 'tis a nasty trick I am serving you, fair Mary. But in the end you won't regret it."

"Come at ten o'clock," said Mary dully. "The door will be unlocked and I shall be waiting in the drawing room."

Blissford smiled down at her and shook his head. "Drawing rooms are so . . . formal. Don't you agree?"

Lady Luck

"Then where?" Mary began. The unfinished sentence hung between them. There was no need to complete it, for they both knew exactly where Lord Blissford meant to meet her.

-Thirteen-

LADY DORSET SLIPPED back into the room with Lord Blissford behind her, he wearing a satisfied grin, she looking as if her best friend had just died. Her husband, who was normally more astute, did not notice their facial expressions, he only saw that they were together after obviously enjoying a cozy tête-à-tête on the balcony. He strode up to them, his face a cold mask, and took his wife's arm. "I think it is time we were going, my dear," he said.

"Yes, Jeremy," said Mary meekly, and let him lead her away.

"I hope I did not interrupt anything," said Dorset between clenched teeth.

"Of course you did not," said Mary, stung. She knew how it must look, but her husband's lack of faith in her hurt all the same. She wished she could explain to him, but how could she?

"I suppose you merely wished for some fresh air," continued Dorset.

Was he trying to pick a quarrel right here in their hostess's salon? She would not allow him to humiliate her so. "I think we had best wait to discuss this until we are home," she said tightly.

"As you wish," he replied.

Amanda was duly found and Lord Dorset whisked his ladies away from the party and home. It was a silent carriage ride, and Amanda, feeling the brewing storm, beat a hasty retreat to her room. Mary, too, tried to escape, but her husband followed.

They were barely in the door to her room when a small brown animal rushed at his lordship's boot, growling. Dorset grabbed a bed pillow and flung it on the little dog. Mary gasped as the animal yelped and scurried under the bed. Dorset turned angrily to her. "What is there between you and Blissford?" he demanded.

"Nothing!" she cried. "But even if there were, what would it matter to you?"

Her husband looked at her so fiercely she thought her bones would melt. In two quick strides he was in front of her. He grabbed her in a rough embrace and locked his lips over hers. She could feel the cloth of his coat through her thin gown, feel his heart beating, and she suddenly ached for him. But before she could put her arms around his neck, he pushed her from him. "I'll not be cuckolded by any man," he declared. As if suddenly drained of his energy reserves, he swayed.

"Jeremy!" she cried, and moved to help him, but he held her off and took a deep breath.

"I shall bid you good night," he said coldly, and left her to collapse sobbing onto her bed. The little pug crept out from its hiding place and jumped up beside her. Whimpering, it nuzzled under her arm. "Oh, Rufus," she sobbed. And the mention of her husband's middle name only made her cry all the harder.

After some time she pulled herself together and made her way to Amanda's room, thinking all the while how very wrong things had turned out. She should have married Mr. Amhearst. Too late for such musings, she told herself stoically. She must live the life she had chosen, live with the decisions she had made. The die was cast. No matter what else her husband now thought of her, she would not have him think her a thief. She would make sure the Dorset necklace was returned.

She went to Amanda's room and tapped on her door. Amanda was already ready for bed, her maid long dismissed. She blinked in surprise at the sight of her cousin, who put a finger to her lips and slipped inside. "I was unable to get the missing heirloom tonight. You will have to help me yet again."

"But how can I help?" asked Amanda.

"You must go to the opera tomorrow night with Jeremy. I shall pretend illness and stay home. Lord Blissford is to bring it to me tomorrow night."

"I don't understand," said Amanda. "Why does Lord Blissford not just bring it to you during the day? Why all this secrecy?"

"I cannot explain," said Mary. "But you must promise to help me in this, Amanda. I must recover that necklace before my husband discovers it is gone."

Amanda shrugged. "Very well. Going to the opera does not sound such a very hard thing to do."

"Thank you," said Mary, and returned to her own room. She rang for her abigail and, while she awaited Randall's arrival, sat before her looking glass and mentally poked at her wounds, reliving the last two days. What could she have done differently? Should she have confessed all to Jeremy to begin with, thrown herself on his mercy? Surely he could have recovered the necklace. Lord Blissford's earlier words came back to haunt her: "Do you really think he cares so much that he would forgive you its loss?" She no longer knew what to think.

Her lower lip began to tremble and a tear slipped from the corner of her eye. Another tear followed and then another.

By the time her maid arrived, her face was very wet and her eyes very red. "My lady! What is wrong?"

"Nothing," sobbed Mary, throwing herself on the dressing table and burying her head in her arms.

Randall knelt beside her mistress and put an arm around her. "Oh, dear! I shall fetch his lordship."

"No!" cried Mary, sitting up and grabbing her arm. Randall stood rooted, staring at her mistress in alarm. "His lordship cannot help me," said Mary. "No one can help me. Tomorrow night I must sell myself to Lord Blissford for the price of an emerald necklace." She burst into fresh tears, and once the whole terrible story came out, tears filled her abigail's eyes as well.

"Perhaps you should tell his lordship all," said Randall at last as she readied Mary for bed.

Mary shook her head. "There is no way I can redeem myself in his eyes," she said sadly. "He already thinks the worst of Lord Blissford and me." She shook her head. "I loved him so."

"Lord Blissford?" Randall was frankly shocked.

Mary smiled ruefully. "No. Jeremy." She sighed.

"He did not love me at the start. And now he does not love me at the end."

Randall could find no comforting words for her mistress and left her at last to sob herself to sleep.

Mary could not bring herself to go downstairs to breakfast the next morning. The thought of facing her husband was more than she could bear. She had hot chocolate sent to her room then went to check on Sir Percy. He smiled at her as she entered his room. "How are you feeling today?" she asked.

"Better, thank you. Still weak as a kitten, though."

"You will be hale and hearty soon," promised Mary. "Do you feel up to eating any breakfast?"

Sir Percy nodded.

"Good. I shall see some is sent up to you." Mary turned to go.

"Er, Mary." She turned to see a red-faced Sir Percy. "Is Miss Tuttle, that is, was she able to pay her gambling debts?"

Mary thought sadly of the high cost of Miss Tuttle's gambling debts. "Yes. It has all been taken care of."

Belowstairs, Miss Tuttle and Aubrey were trying to work out the details of their elopement.

"What do you mean we cannot elope while Mary and Dorset are at the opera?" demanded Aubrey.

"Mary has asked me to accompany him," said Amanda. "It is very important, for she is getting the necklace back from Lord Blissford this evening."

"Why the devil can't the fellow simply bring the thing 'round during the day?" demanded Aubrey irritably.

"I don't know," said Amanda. "I asked Mary that very question myself and she would not say. She only said she is going to pretend to be ill and that I must go to the opera with her husband. Is it not strange?"

Aubrey scratched his head and thought for a moment. The answer to the mystery of his stepsister's peculiar behavior suddenly came to him. "So that is how the land lays," he said. "Of course! She and Blissford had been thick as thieves even before Dorset returned." Amanda looked at him, puzzled. "Never mind," he told her. "I shall go to the opera, too, and we can elope after we return home. I will have Vayne's carriage standing right 'round the corner."

Amanda clapped her hands. "How exciting! I can hardly wait for tonight."

* * *

The Earl of Dorset could hardly wait for the night as well. He didn't know what had happened to his family's heirloom necklace. It had not made its appearance at any jewelry shop. Something had happened to it. Of that much he was sure. He was equally sure that something had happened between his wife and Blissford. Had they had an assignation when he was sick? Dorset glared at his looking glass and yanked his cravat from his throat, throwing it onto the floor where two others lay. He took another cloth from his valet and began again the meticulous winding and knotting, wishing it was Lord Blissford's throat between his hands. The fellow would not have Mary, even if it meant taking her to the continent to keep her from him. He would win her before this night was over, he vowed. Dorset's eyes narrowed. And if he could not win her, he would take her.

The earl went down to dinner. He had barely gotten inside the drawing room when a footman presented him with a note from his wife. He crumpled it and, excusing himself, marched from the room while Aubrey and Amanda exchanged knowing glances. Taking the stairs two at a time, he went to Mary's bedroom and burst in.

She was lying in her bed. She sat up at the

sight of him, her eyes wide with fear, then fell back on her pillows.

He came to the bedside and looked icily down at her. "You are felling ill, my dear?" Indeed, she looked white as a ghost and there was a thin film of perspiration on her brow.

Her lip began to tremble. "I am afraid so," she said in a weak voice. "I beg you not to change your plans. Amanda has been so looking forward to the opera." She blinked several times and at last turned her head.

He took her chin and turned her face back to him. Tears were coursing down her cheeks. What did he see in her eyes? Fear? he asked himself. Dear God. No woman had ever before been afraid of him. What kind of monster was he turning into? Suddenly the earl felt the cruelest of villains. He knelt by the bed. "Mary, dear."

She pressed a hand to her mouth and turned her head away. "I am so sorry," she sobbed.

"Please don't be," he said. "There will be other operas, other evenings out."

Now she began to cry in earnest, turning her face into her pillow. The earl watched helplessly. "Shall I send for the doctor?"

"No!" cried Mary. They sat for a moment, each one searching the other's face for the answer to an unspoken question. If Mary had not really been ill before, she indeed felt so now. Her restless night combined with her present tears were causing her head to throb painfully. She rubbed her forehead and said, "I promise I shall feel better by tomorrow."

"You are most likely exhausted from nursing us all," said Dorset. He kissed her forehead. "Rest. I shall check on you when I return home."

And by the time you have returned home I shall have the necklace, thought Mary. And a lover.

Shortly after dinner the earl left for the opera with Miss Tuttle and Mr. Mayhill, and the servants settled down to enjoy their evening meal. All except Randall, who had watched his lordship leave from an upstairs window. She furtively made her way to the room where Sir Percy lay. She tapped timidly at his door and, on being bid to enter, bit her lip and bravely went inside. Sir Percy looked at her in surprise and she bobbed him a curtsy. "I beg your pardon," she said. "I am so sorry to disturb you, but my mistress is in trouble and I didn't dare send anyone else to tell you, as I am sure she wants no one to know." Sir Percy was still looking perplexed. "I am Randall," she explained. "Her ladyship's abigail. She is in terrible trouble."

Sir Percy gulped. "Trouble?" he parroted.

Randall tried to give him as thorough an

explanation as time and modesty allowed. "You must hurry and fetch his lordship home," she finished, "for I know she doesn't wish to do this thing, and if he does not return in time, it will be too late."

"Yes," agreed Sir Percy, throwing off his blankets and bounding out of bed. "I shall take care of it." He swayed and put a hand to his head.

"Oh, dear," gasped Randall. "I will get someone to help you."

"No time," said Sir Percy. "I shall dress myself. Go on to your mistress and tell her not to worry."

Randall went to her mistress but decided it was best to tell her nothing.

Sir Percy was dressed in less than ten minutes. His cravat was sloppily tied and his waistcoat buttoned wrong, but for the first time in his life he took no interest. In five more minutes he was at his cousin's stable, tapping his toe impatiently while the stable boy saddled his lordship's favorite horse.

Lord Dorset guided his party through the throng at the opera house. They were halfway to their box when they encountered the dowager Lady Dorset in the company of a tall, handsome man with gray hair. "Good evening, Mother," said his lordship.

"Jeremy." Her ladyship presented her cheek to be kissed. She greeted Amanda and Aubrey. "But where is Mary?" she asked.

"She was not feeling well," said Dorset.

His mother raised an eyebrow. "Really?"

Her son gave her a puzzled look.

Amanda squirmed uncomfortably. "Should we not be getting to our box?" she asked.

"Yes, of course," said his lordship, and they moved on.

The curtain had barely gone up on the first act when Sir Percy made his appearance. "Percy! What the devil are you doing here?" whispered his lordship. He regarded his cousin's cravat with horror. "And who dressed you?"

"A word with you," said Sir Percy, nodding to the curtain.

His lordship followed him out of the box. "What is the matter? Has anything happened to Mary?"

"Not yet," said Sir Percy. "But you had best return home before something does."

"What!" exclaimed Dorset.

"Sssh." Percy looked nervously about them. "I'll explain on the way. Come on, man."

"All right," said his lordship. He reentered the box. "I am afraid I must leave," he announced.

"No!" cried Amanda, and then blushed as

several pairs of curious eyes turned toward her. "The opera has just begun. You cannot leave."

"You and Aubrey may stay and watch it. I shall send the carriage back for you," said his lordship, and was gone.

Amanda turned a worried face to Aubrey, who shrugged philosophically. "We tried," he said. An expression of delight dawned on his face. "Now we can elope earlier," he said. "We'll take a chair back, pop into Vayne's carriage, and be on our way."

"As you wish," agreed Amanda. "The opera bores me, anyway."

Mary sat gloomily in her chair while Randall put up her hair. She was sure Lord Blissford expected her to meet him wearing a peignoir and with her hair down, but she refused. She would end up the evening as his paramour, but she was determined to begin it as a lady of principle.

Randall finally finished her ministrations. "You look lovely," she said, then blushed for her thoughtless remark.

"Thank you," said her ladyship listlessly. "You may leave."

Randall left her staring at her looking glass and seeing an empty future. The house settled

into quiet and she slipped downstairs and un-
latched the front door. With heavy steps she
climbed the stairs back to her room. It seemed
she had barely gotten inside it when she thought
she heard the door downstairs open.

-Fourteen-

IT LACKED TEN minutes till the magic hour of ten o'clock when Lord Blissford mounted the steps of the Dorset town house. He judged that his rival should be stuck listening to Catalani's caterwauling for at least another hour. Of course, once the curtain had come down at the King's Theatre they would have to fight the fashionable crowd, make conversation, wait for their carriage to be brought 'round. It would be easily another hour and a half before Dorset came home. Plenty of time for a leisurely, enjoyable seduction.

Blissford tried the door. The lady had been as good as her word. He opened it and slipped in. He wished he had had the foresight to ask the exact location of her room. Ah, well. Most of these houses were similarly laid out and his lordship felt sure an educated guess would bring him to the correct boudoir.

He stopped in front of the most likely door, his heart pounding with excitement, and tapped gently. He thought he heard a faint "Come in," and entered. The heavy velvet curtains at the window were drawn and a lone candle cast a feeble light on the far side of the room. His lordship stood for a moment, allowing his eyes to grow accustomed to the dark. He saw a form huddled under the bedcovers and grinned lecherously. "There is no need to hide, sweetheart," he said. "I shall be gentle."

Sweetheart threw off the covers and rose from the bed like Neptune rising out of the sea. "I wish I could make the same promise," growled Lord Dorset, and leveled a pistol at the intruder.

Lord Blissford let out a startled yelp before recovering himself. "Dorset," he stammered.

"Surprised to see me here?" inquired the earl. "I suppose you thought me at the opera."

"It would have been so much more convenient if you were," admitted Blissford.

"I believe you have something I want," said Dorset.

"As do you," replied the other man.

"I am afraid my wife does not want you," said his lordship.

"Oh?" Lord Blissford looked frankly disbelieving.

"I see you do not believe me. Perhaps we should let the lady speak for herself," suggested Lord Dorset. "Mary!" he called.

Mary entered the room and both men fastened their gaze on her. "Mary, tell his lordship whom you will have," said Dorset.

Mary looked steadily at Lord Blissford. "I will have Jeremy," she said.

"I don't believe it!" cried Lord Blissford. "You say that merely because he has forced you to."

"I say it because it is true. I am sorry if I misled you early in our friendship. And I am even sorrier that you felt obliged to trick me."

His lordship's chin went up with this accusation. "I can assure you I would never have served you such a trick had I not felt that deep down . . ." His lordship cast a look at Dorset and left his sentence unfinished. "Are we to duel or do you shoot me down where I stand."

"You deserve to be shot where you stand," said Dorset. "But no. We do neither. I'll thank you for the return of my wife's necklace."

Lord Blissford smiled a cocky smile. He reached inside his coat pocket and pulled out a long slim box and tossed it on the bed. "You are quite welcome," he said.

"And how much do I owe you?" asked Dorset lightly.

Lord Blissford smiled the smile of a good loser. "Nothing," he replied. "Consider it . . . a wedding present."

"I'll say this for you, Blissford. You're a curst good sport."

Lord Blissford shrugged. "When the game is over, 'tis over. No need to show me out. I shall find my way." He bowed to his rival. At the door he stopped and took Mary's hand. "Your husband is a lucky man," he said, and kissed her fingertips.

Mary stood a moment, watching him make his way down the hallway. She felt rather than saw her husband next to her.

"Regrets?" he asked.

"How can you ask such a thing?" replied Mary.

"I have been less than a husband—no, less than a friend to you. I should not blame you if in my absence you had found someone you preferred," said his lordship humbly. "There was little enough time to speak of this before Blissford came. You were upset, concerned for the necklace. But I wish you to look deeply into your heart and examine it. Let me ask you again, and you may be honest with me, I assure you. I should not blame you if you'd found someone else to love. 'Tis no less than I deserve." Mary

188

opened her mouth, but he rushed on before she could speak, anxious to be done with his speech. "Do you want Blissford? For if you prefer him, I shall call him back this minute. I'll leave this house, leave London, return to the continent."

Mary put a hand to his cheek. "Oh, Jeremy. There never has been, never will be, anyone I prefer over you."

He clasped her to him and kissed her.

"Is everything all right?" came a familiar voice. "Oh."

Lord Dorset and Mary looked to see a blushing Sir Percival backing away down the hallway. "It looks as though things are all settled. I'm off to bed. Rather fagged. I'll be on my way home tomorrow. Good luck, er, good night."

Mary giggled and her husband kicked the door shut. He scooped her up in his arms and carried her to her bed. He laid her on it and stood for a moment looking down at her. What a gorgeous creature she was, inside as well as out. When he thought of what she had been willing to do simply to retrieve his family necklace . . . "I was a fool not to see what a treasure I had all along," he murmured.

She smiled bravely up at him, obviously nervous about the unknown experience that lay ahead but ready to give whatever he asked. Poor thing, he thought. She had waited a long time for her wedding night. He smiled and slid onto the bed next to her. "Don't worry, sweetheart. I'll be gentle," he whispered, and she giggled again. He planted a kiss on her throat.

A knock on the door prevented him from going further. He looked up in irritation. "Who is it?" he demanded.

"Blissford," came a muffled voice. The earl swore and clambered off the bed. He stomped to the door and threw it open.

"I thought, perhaps, before leaving I ought to mention an unusual encounter I had in front of your house just now."

-Fifteen-

"WERE YOUR BROTHER-IN-LAW and Miss Tuttle, perhaps, planning to leave town to visit friends or relatives?" asked Lord Blissford.

"What the devil are you talking about?" demanded the earl.

Blissford shrugged. "I just met them outside getting into a carriage bearing your cousin's crest. The gentleman was carrying a portmanteau. Perhaps Sir Percival is removing to the country and Miss Tuttle and Mr. Mayhill accompany him?" he suggested sarcastically.

Lord Dorset's eyes narrowed. "Perhaps that is so. I will bid you good night, sir." He slammed the door on Lord Blissford, who again shrugged and strolled off whistling.

"What did Lord Blissford say? He saw Amanda and Aubrey?" asked Mary as he rejoined her on the bed.

"Nothing. Just another ruse to get me away. Now," he said, running a hand along her arm. "Where were we?" He took her earlobe between his lips.

"What if they are eloping?" worried Mary.

"Then we must wish them well, for a couple more deserving of each other I have never seen."

Mary sat up. "Perhaps Amanda left a note." She scrambled off the bed and her lord frowned. She ran down the hall to Amanda's room, Dorset following reluctantly behind. A moment later she came out, her face white, her hand holding a piece of cream-colored vellum. "They have eloped," she cried. "Oh, Jeremy! We must do something. You must go find them." Even as her husband was protesting that it couldn't be true, she ran to Sir Percy's door and banged on it.

He opened the door, resplendent in a maroon-colored brocade dressing gown. "What's to do?" he asked.

"Amanda and Aubrey have eloped," said Mary.

"How could they elope?" objected the earl. "I left them at the opera. And they didn't even have a carriage." He paused and looked at his cousin, who looked back at him.

"When I was sick," said Percy slowly. Understanding dawned. "My carriage!" he roared. "He took Miss Tuttle! In *my* carriage!"

The earl swore and stomped off down the hall in search of his boots. "Get your clothes on, Percy," he called. "We leave in ten minutes."

Mary followed him into her room and watched him pull on his boots. "Will you be able to find them?" she asked in a small voice.

"Of course," said his lordship. "We know where they're bound and they only have a few minutes' head start. We shall be back within the hour. I hope Miss Tuttle's mama will consider Aubrey a good match." He strode to his wife and hooked an arm around her. Smiling down at her, he asked, "Can you wait for your neglectful husband yet a little longer?"

She nodded and tried to smile.

"Don't worry, love. All will end well. You shall see."

Ten minutes later the two men were out the door, a tearful Mary waving them good-bye.

An hour later they returned with the miscreants in tow, Aubrey looking surly and Amanda pouting. "Ah, my dear," said his lordship, coming to kiss his wife. "You may congratulate your brother and Miss Tuttle. They are engaged to be married."

"And so we would have been if you hadn't stopped us," said Aubrey.

"Aubrey! How could you have been so thoughtless?" cried his sister.

"Thoughtless! I put a great deal of thought into this. Had the whole thing worked out," said Aubrey resentfully.

"It would have been absolutely scandalous," scolded Mary. "Think of what it would have done to Amanda's reputation, and how grieved her mama would have been."

"Better than marrying Norton," said Aubrey.

"Norton? Who said she was to marry Norton?" demanded the earl.

"You did," accused Aubrey.

"I did nothing of the sort," said Dorset.

"He was going to offer for me," put in Amanda.

"I wasn't going to make you marry him if you didn't want to, you little fool," snapped the earl. He shook his head impatiently.

"It will be ever so much better this way," soothed Mary. "Only think. If you had eloped, you would not have been able to have a proper wedding or a wedding gown or a wedding breakfast."

Amanda looked thoughtful. "That is true," she said.

The earl turned his scorn on his brother-in-law. "And how did you propose to support a wife when you've not yet attained your majority?" he demanded.

"I should have found a way," said Aubrey sullenly.

"Well, it is fortunate for you I have already found you a way," said his lordship. "I have bought you a commission in the cavalry."

Aubrey's eyes lit up. "A commission? Oh, smashing! I say, Dorset, that is good of you."

The earl shrugged off his brother-in-law's gratitude. "Not much excitement now. But who knows? Boney could escape. Then you'd see some action."

Aubrey turned to Amanda. "How do you like that? A military life. We shall travel, see the world."

Amanda pronounced herself well pleased with the arrangement.

"Good," said his lordship. "That is all settled. Now perhaps we may retire for the night?"

The others agreed. Mary shepherded Amanda out of the room, Aubrey close behind. Sir Percy was about to follow.

"Percy, old fellow."

Sir Percy turned and looked at his cousin.

"You look the very devil," said the earl.

"Still weak as a kitten," confessed Percy.

"I am sorry about the way things turned out. I know how fond you are of Miss Tuttle."

"Well, yes," agreed Percy slowly. "But to tell the truth, I'm beginning to think she might be a bit of a handful."

His lordship smiled at this understatement.

"Just a bit," he agreed. He clapped his cousin on the back. "Let's go find our beds."

The two men went upstairs, Sir Percy to his room to collapse, the earl to try once again to make love to his wife. He stepped inside the bedroom door and Rufus rushed at him. Dorset rolled his eyes as the pug growled and mangled his boot. "I thought you had put him away," he complained.

Mary rushed to rescue her husband's foot. She spanked the pug on the nose. "No, Rufus! Naughty." She smiled playfully up at her husband. "He just needs time to get to know you," she said. "I am sure he will come to love you."

"I shall have to work on winning his affection," said the earl. He held out his hand for the dog to sniff. Rufus growled and snapped at him. "Ah, well. Some things take time." He sighed and smiled at his wife. "It took over three years to bring your husband to heel. I imagine I cannot expect Rufus to change overnight."

Mary set the little dog down and it trotted off and settled itself on the hearth rug.

The earl removed his boots and tossed them to the dog. "Those should keep you happy," he told it. He turned to his wife.

She smiled shyly at him. "Thank you," she said.

"For helping Aubrey?" The earl dismissed his valiant deed with a shrug.

"Not just Aubrey." A pretty flush decorated the delicate face. "All of us," she said.

The earl grinned widely at her. All his dragons lay vanquished outside the castle walls. Now, at long last, he could claim the princess. Slowly he reached up and began to pull the pins from her hair, watching the lovely dark tresses fall to her shoulders. All the pins out, he stopped to admire his handiwork. He took a handful of the soft, dark stuff and put it to his face. It smelled of lavender and he brushed his lips with the soft tresses. He looked down at Mary. She stood regarding him, a look of breathless anticipation on her flushed face, her lips slightly parted. He kissed them, reveling in their softness. Once more the earl picked up his wife and laid her on the bed. Smiling down at her, he ran a gentle hand over her soft curves and whispered, "I, Jeremy, take thee, Mary. . . ."

The dowager Lady Dorset sat in her box at the Royal Opera House, half listening to the man who lounged next to her. She let her gaze roam the theater. In one box she saw Sir Percival Vayne with a middle-aged couple and a demure-looking young lady with brown curls. Sir Percy was grinning at her in a way only a man on the edge of infatuation could.

In another box her ladyship saw Lord and Lady Wexford. The golden-haired Lord Blissford sat next to Lady Wexford. He said something to the lady and she laughed and rapped him with her fan. Lord Blissford smiled. His eyes fell on the occupants of a box nearby, and for a moment his expression turned wistful.

The dowager followed his gaze to the couple in the box. The man was a handsome fellow with a straight nose and a strong chin and a fine pair of brown eyes. The woman next to him was nothing short of exquisite. A doe-eyed creature with a long, graceful neck. On that neck glittered an elaborately worked necklace of emeralds and pearls.

As if feeling the dowager's eyes on her, the young woman looked in her direction. She smiled at her mother-in-law. The dowager knew that smile, for she had worn it herself when she was Mary's age. It was the smile of a contented woman.

The curtain came down and her ladyship's companion turned to her. "A most satisfying ending, wouldn't you say?" he observed.

She smiled. "It most certainly is," she said.

427